Alexander Rekemchuk

BOYS WHO DID A-SINGING GO

A novel

Fredonia Books
Amsterdam, The Netherlands

Boys Who Did A-Singing Go
A Novel

by
Alexander Rekemchuk
Translated from the Russian Katherine Judelson
Designed by Lev Katayev

ISBN 1-58963-046-7

Reprinted from the 1972 edition

Fredonia Books
Amsterdam, The Netherlands
http://www.FredoniaBooks.com

PART ONE

1

When I go out into the big wide world, as the saying goes, when I start to earn my own living and have a place of my own, the first thing I shall do is get a dog. For I owe my life to a dog....

Of course when it comes to the point, I really owe it to my parents: my father Gennady Prokhorov was a captain in the army and my mother Tamara Prokhorova was an army doctor. They married during World War II and after it was over they settled in the town of Ashkhabad where their unit was stationed and it was there that I was born.

On the night of October 6, 1948 a great earthquake shook Ashkhabad: the town was laid waste and countless people were buried in the rubble, my parents among them. As luck would have it, they fought through the whole war without being hit by a single bullet and then in the middle of peace-time a collapsing wall crushed them as they lay peacefully asleep in the middle of the night.

But how was it then that I escaped and am still alive to tell the tale? For I was with them that night, sleeping in my cot in the very same room. Of course I myself don't remember anything about the catastrophe, anything at all, neither the earthquake, nor my unfortunate parents, nor my miraculous escape. I was less than two at the time.

Later though I was to hear the whole story from a woman, who came to visit me at the orphanage and knew all the details, for she had been working in the same outfit as my parents.

She brought me a pile of goodies, all kinds of sweets and honey-cakes and afterwards, wiping away her tears the while, she told me the following story.

It appeared there had been another member of the family, an Alsatian by the name of Rex. As is expected of dogs he had been a faithful servant of his masters but was particularly attached to me although I was still quite tiny; my parents actually left me in his care when they were not at home.

On that fateful night when the inhabitants of Ashkhabad were still fast asleep, in the last few seconds before the earthquake the dog heard the rumbling deep down in the earth (animals always hear such things well ahead of human beings and sense the approach of disaster much earlier), at which he jumped into my cot, took hold of my vest in his teeth and leapt through the window that was wide open because the night was so close. Seconds later the house collapsed.

That was how a dog saved my life. I've been told that people in Ashkhabad tell each other the story of that amazing rescue to this day.

But what happened after that? I was sent to a children's reception centre, not in Ashkhabad itself, but in Lipetsk: there were so many earthquake orphans like me that we were sent to different towns to be taken care of.

It turned out actually that my parents did have some relatives: various uncles and aunts appeared in Ashkhabad after the earthquake so as to divide up among themselves the few belongings that could be retrieved from under the rubble. However not one of them expressed the wish to take me under his wing, apparently considering that the state was in a much better position to make a respectable citizen of me, and as far as I can judge, they were not far wrong.

It was the woman who came to see me in Lipetsk who told me about them as well. Apart from the sweets and the honey-cakes she also brought me a photograph of my father and mother: it shows them standing side by side in uniform complete with medals, very young and smiling. On the back of the photo the woman had written the address of the cemetery where my parents were buried and the number of their graves, so that when I grew up and visited my home town I could go there.

I treasure that photograph, not only because it is all I have to remember my father and mother by, and not only because as soon as I finish school and start working and have enough money for such a long journey I shall make a point of going to Ashkhabad and finding my parents' graves.

No, you see, there's another reason as well. Orphanage children like me are obsessed with their parents. From the very first that is the question that bothers them more than anything else. Who were they? Why aren't they there? Where have they got to? No one ever believes or can bring himself to believe that his parents—his mother or his father—could have simply turned their backs on their child, left him in a station waiting room or abandoned him in a porch somewhere. Or simply turned up at a reception centre and handed over a tiny bundle saying: here you are, hang onto him, we don't need him, we've got other plans.

When it comes to the point though, this is the kind of thing that has happened in most cases. But Heaven help the person who so much as hints to any one of us that he is a mere foundling. The smaller children would bite you and the bigger ones would bash your face in.

That kind of start in the world is not to anyone's taste: no one wants to despise the human race from his cradle.

This is why any orphanage child knows even more about his ancestors than those who have grown up under their parents' roof without a care in the world. He knows everything, every detail: some lost their parents in the war, others' parents died at sea and others' tried out dangerous innoculations on themselves to further scientific experiments which unhappily did not work out.

Nine out of ten of these stories are pure fiction, inventions thought up by the children themselves. There is no end to the things they dream up.

I expect you wonder why I am going into all this?

I just want to be sure no suspicion attaches to my story. For perhaps somebody might think that my own story sounds too far-fetched to be true. Yet I have the photo here before me now. I always have it with me and on the back you can read the number of the graves and the address....

By the way that woman who came to visit me also left me the addresses of my aunts and uncles. It was probably so that I should write to them and remember them at holiday times.

But one thing that the woman was unable to tell me and that I still do not know to this day, but would very much like to (I would give anything in the world to find out) is what became of the dog, the Alsatian called Rex to whom I owe my life.

Whatever became of him?

Of course in those tense difficult days after the earthquake nobody would have had time to bother about homeless dogs, when there were so many homeless people to attend to. As likely as not no one gave them a thought.

Yet what *did* happen I wonder to that fine dog after he lost his masters? I expect he wandered around the town with nothing to eat and howling at night. . . . I like to think that he was taken in by some kind people. Or still better that some of the border guards in the mountains or some militia-men had given him a home, for they know how to treat dogs. Then I would feel happy about Rex. But if. . . . Sometimes I meet stray dogs roaming the streets or backyards looking for scraps in stinking rubbish dumps. When they see passers-by they give a little wave of their tails as if to say: don't be afraid of me, on you go, I won't bite—but at the same time they sidle away, backing timidly up against a wall, ready to take to their heels in case a passer-by should bend down to pick up a stone to throw at them.

The first holiday I get after I start working I shall go and spend in Ashkhabad and the first pay-packet I get I shall use to buy an Alsatian, an Alsatian puppy and I shall call him Rex.

* * *

I shall not have to wait long for that opportunity now. I'm not far off seventeen. Once I get my school leaving certificate then off I go wherever I please.

I could of course try and join the army of students—perhaps I might get in. But that would mean more studying, more sitting around on hostel beds and struggling to make ends meet with a grant of twenty rubles a month.

No, I really have had enough of that for the moment.

How much more attractive it is to think of setting off to some magnificent place far away, like the one an old friend of mine has settled in and tells me about in his rare letters. He says that life out there is great, the lads he's with are a good crowd and the girls are out of this world! What's more he clears two hundred and fifty a month.

Why shouldn't I do the same? All it needs is for me, a young man in search of romantic adventure, to jump on a train and puff-puff . . . and unknown horizons will spread wide before me and then will come my first success, first recognition, first love and first disappointment. . . .

Now doesn't that sound wonderful!

But what if—you can take it or leave it, whichever you prefer—if I've tasted all that already though I'm not yet seventeen.

I have. All of it.

The distant travels, first success and recognition, first disappointment and first love. Second love as well.

And what if—although I'm still not seventeen yet—I know that every gift which fortune could shower on me has already come my way, that they are not there to be looked forward to but already belong to the past?

So that sounds funny? It may do for some people, but for me there's nothing funny about it at all. It's something I don't even like talking about.

I'd much rather put on a record. Admittedly my record player isn't up to much and the turntable squeaks; what's more it isn't even mine but belongs to the school. The record's terribly worn as well and rasps from start to finish because I'm always listening to it, but on the other hand the record does belong to me. It's a record that has seen better days, it's already four years old. But you can still hear something though.

Here we go. First comes the introduction, then the orchestral accompaniment starts up; the tempo quickens and the music crescendos. Then come the words:

With a roar, roar, roar,
The propellers start to spin;
Then we soar, soar, soar
Those azure heights to win. . .

It's hard for the singer to tackle as well, for the song starts low in his range, springing up from the earth as it were; for a high voice its harder to start low down than to start off with high notes.

Then the orchestra changes key and the same melody is repeated a third higher. The melody soars up and up to almost incredible heights—incredible for a man's voice. It would be out of reach for many a soprano but that's the whole point—this song isn't being sung by a woman. A woman's voice would have been all wrong for this song of masculine endeavour.

I suppose I must turn down the volume though because there are small boys asleep in the next room, boys from Form III who I'm meant to be supervising during the rest-hour, when kids are made to go to sleep in broad daylight and of course have no wish to do so and quietly get up to mischief, telling each other jokes, laughing and stifling their guffaws in their pillows, but as soon as you go into the room their eyes are all shut tight as if they were fast asleep and some of them are even starting up with a snore.

I'm in charge of those Young Pioneers. It's

holiday time at the moment, but alas the holidays are almost over, it's already the last week in August.

This summer we've spent near Vereya again: it's a small old town, but if you haven't been there and don't know it, you're not missing much. But the countryside here isn't bad at all. There's a small river called the Protva and then come endless woods and there's a big orchard in the grounds of our Young Pioneer camp.

In fact there's an apple tree under my very window and the apples on it are ripe already. There are lots of them and the kids are allowed to pick them: we make the most of this and eat as many as we can find room for. We munch away, but it's almost as if we hadn't touched the tree because there's such a bumper crop this year. The whole of Vereya and all the surrounding countryside is full of apple trees, apple trees and still more apple trees. The local kids throw apples at each other instead of stones and for some reason you can always see apples floating down the river Protva....

Let the antennae,
antennae,
antennae
Tune into the voice of Earth;
Starwards Antey[1]*,*
Antey,
Antey,
Fly on for all you are worth...

But to go back to the apple tree that grows under my window. When we came out here at the very beginning of the summer all the apple

---

[1] Large Soviet freight plane first produced in the 1960s. —*Tr.*

trees were still in flower. My apple tree too was a mass of white blossoms, each one of them holding out the promise of an apple to come. When I looked at that canopy of white blossoms with just a blush of pink about them I thought to myself however many apples will there be on this one tree? A million.

Then the blossoms disappeared and in place of each one there appeared a little globe; these quickly swelled and soon started to look like miniature apples. Of course they weren't ready to eat at that stage, horribly bitter, enough to make your eyes water. But each day those little globes grew just that bit bigger.

But later I noticed how the tree started shedding some of them before they had grown into apples. At night-time when there wasn't even a breath of wind I used to hear them falling in my sleep. When I woke up there would be a ring of them all round the tree as far as the branches stretched.

At first I suspected that some of the kids had been up to mischief just shaking the tree for the hell of it, to have some fun as boys will, for those bitter little green balls used to fairly rain down. But the boys gave me their word of honour that it had nothing to do with them and their word is something I take seriously.

Then I grew concerned at the thought that perhaps the tree had been attacked by some kind of disease, and went to see the gardener whom we called Yerofeich. I told him what had been happening and led him over to take a look at the apple tree.

"No," he said looking at the tree and the windfalls, "there's nothing wrong with the tree. No need to worry."

"But why do so many fall then?"

"But, don't you see, son," answered Yerofeich with a sigh, "Nature always allows a wide margin. Just in case. . . . The frost might have spoiled the blossoms, or they might have been battered to bits by hail. Then birds might have pecked at the embryos. But this summer none of that happened, we've been lucky with the weather."

"Yes," I said, nodding in agreement.

"So, there you are. Now if all those apples had survived and ripened the tree would have been done for. It couldn't have stood the weight, the branches would have broken off. So the apple tree itself gets rid of the surplus, shaking it off in advance so that it can stand the weight of the ripe fruit at the end. D'you understand?"

"Yes," I replied.

"That's all right then," said the gardener bringing the conversation to an end. "So don't you worry. Everything's just as it should be. There'll be enough apples from this tree for you and all the young rascals, as many as you could wish for. It's a good summer we're having."

He was right, was old Yerofeich.

The apple tree was right, too, to have got rid of all the surplus. Even now it's still laden with full, ripe, bright red apples with a delicious flavour.

Starwards Antey,
Antey,
Antey,
Fly on for all you are worth. . .

That's enough for today. I must take care of the record. It's not to be found in any of the shops any more nowadays.

By the way, it's my record; not mine in the

sense that it doesn't belong to the school as the record-player does, but in quite a different sense. . . .

The voice on that record is mine. It belongs to me—Zhenya Prokhorov.

2

There were lots of trees down there in Lipetsk[1] too. I can remember the apple, cherry and bird-cherry blossom. But in those days I was hard put to it to tell one tree from another. Probably the most common trees in that part of the world were limes and I expect the name Lipetsk comes from the word for lime tree.

Those trees I can still remember quite clearly, enormous with their wide spreading branches shutting out the sky overhead.

But taken all in all there's very little that I remember about the part of my life that belongs to the orphanage, except one or two quite unimportant things.

There's an expression "threads of memory" and in my case the very beginning of that thread proved very simple, nothing other than an actual piece of white cotton thread, the white cotton our flannel orphanage blankets were hemmed with. At night I used to cover myself up with one of those blankets and go fast asleep under it, but during our rest-hour (we had a rest-hour at the orphanage as well, of course) it provided me with a wonderful pastime which helped to make the hour pass more quickly. On the quiet I used to unravel the white thread, which was quite a com-

[1] Derived from the word "lipa"—lime tree.—*Tr.*

plicated undertaking because the blanket was hemmed with intricate stitching. It was slow, rather fiddly work and I only managed to do two or three stitches each rest-hour, and there must have been at least a hundred on the blanket—in those days I couldn't count further than a hundred. What was more both ends of the blanket were trimmed in the same fashion, so when the top end was finished you could start work on the end at the bottom of the bed. The job would probably have kept me busy for a long time, a very long time. I could look confidently and calmly into the future as I steadily pursued my unravelling for no changes or abrupt turns of fate were expected in those days.

However I was not destined to finish the blanket I started work on—I only got half-way along the top end before I had to call a halt.

* * *

One fine day we were all assembled in the big hall of the orphanage, where we usually got together for all sorts of games, for dancing or singing and where we also used to do our morning exercises.

It was a large room with walls festooned with paper flags and garlands which we children used to cut out and stick together. There was also a portrait of Vladimir Ulyanov hanging there; it showed a curly-headed boy long before he knew he was going to be Lenin.

It was in that big room that the piano stood, the piano that our music teacher Rosa Mikhailovna used to play on when we had singing or dancing lessons. After those lessons it was always locked up again, though.

It had not always been locked though but inevitably one or another of us failed to resist the temptation and would lift the lid and play a tra-la-la or two on their way through the hall.

I used to have a little strum too, only I didn't do so in passing, on my way through the hall. I climbed up on to the revolving stool, settled myself firmly onto the seat and set to work. I used to pick out with one finger various songs that I had heard on the wireless—there was a speaker-extension in the dormitory. It was thrilling to peck first at the white and then the black keys and make a proper song, except for the words. Of course at the beginning I often used to make mistakes and hit the wrong note, one too high or too low, but when that happened it always made me jump as if someone had pinched me or given me a hard slap on the forehead . . . those kind of things were always happening at the orphanage.

But gradually I learned my way about among all those countless keys; I got to know them all till eventually I knew what an ivory would sound like even before I played it. Then I made another fascinating discovery: that you could play one and the same song at the top, bottom or very middle of the keyboard. The only difference was that if you played it down at the left end of the piano then it sounded as if a stout, bearded man was singing it, while if you played it up at the right end it didn't even remind you of a human voice but of a bird's song, the song of a tiny little bird, like a canary. But in the very middle it always sounded just right.

Then I got bored of picking out songs with just one finger, after all I had lots of other fingers, five on each hand! Why should they be idle? So

I roped them all in for the job. Ten fingers, that meant ten keys, all joining in merrily. At first all I got were the same results as the other children, who used to bang away with the palms of their hands giving no thought to what they were doing: bim, bang, boom—it was enough to make anyone block their ears!

But gradually I sorted things out; sweating with the effort, I groped after the right keys and began linking them together in a kind of chain. That note's right here, but I must get rid of that one, and what about this? Yes, it's right too, just what I needed for full, bright, unbearably resplendent beauty!

I can't really say how far my first acquaintance with the miraculous contraption standing in the hall would have developed because it had to come to an end all too soon. Rosa Mikhailovna complained to the warden that the children had been treating the piano barbarously in her absence and after that it was locked. The lid came down.... It made me sad, but I survived.

But to get back to where I started, on that day we were all led into the hall, drawn up in two rows: then Rosa Mikhailovna opened the piano with a little key and sat down on the stool. Vera Ivanovna, the warden, had also come along, but she quite often used to come along to hear us sing and watch us dance, so there was nothing unusual about that.

What was unusual though was that she had brought along with her a "representative". All grown-ups who came to visit our orphanage were referred to as "representatives". We would be told: "Today you must all be especially quiet and well-behaved at lunch-time because a representative is coming", or "Children, a representative will be coming into the dormitory today so make sure that you are all in your beds and asleep properly with your eyes shut, your right palm underneath your cheek and your left hand stretched out on top of the blanket."

These representatives used to appear from time to time, inspecting our plates of food and having a look at us lying in bed with our eyes shut. They probably came to make sure that we were being well looked after, and that the cooks fed us properly. But there was precious little point in their inspections, because we were looked after well and the cooks did not take any of our share of the food—they used to take their own meals separately out in the kitchen.

But the representative that came that particular day did not inspect the kitchens or put his head round the dormitory door, he went straight into the big hall where we used to dance and sing. He was very tall and wore round spectacles. He was starting to go grey and a little bald. His greying hair had receded a long way as if to add a little extra to his already large forehead. The representative was wearing a grey suit and a blue tie with spots on it.

He sat down on a chair directly opposite us and next to him sat Vera Ivanovna. She asked the representative about something in a low voice and he nodded by way of reply.

Rosa Mikhailovna put her hands ready on the keyboard and the choir let forth at the tops of their voices with:

A little girl went on her way
Wondering through the pine trees.
She wandered one long sunny day
Gathering wild red strawberries.

However, although it was a song which we all knew very well, we somehow didn't manage to keep together. Some children were singing in the same key as Rosa Mikhailovna's accompaniment, but others seemed to be singing way out, deliberately almost—the words were the same but the music was quite different, we were all at sixes and sevens. But after all we were very young and what else was to be expected?

I noticed that while we were singing away about the little girl and her strawberries the representative kept on flinching, his forehead was knit in a pained frown and his mouth stretched as if he was suffering horribly but struggling heroically to master his pain.

Then I noticed that although we were all singing together and in that medley of voices it was quite impossible to pick out one from the rest, all of a sudden the representative would fix his bespectacled stare on first one of us and then another as if he was trying to guess which voice belonged to whom.

It also seemed to me that at one particular moment his gaze lighted on me and for quite some time it was me to whom those round all-seeing spectacles were glued.

"And now," said Rosa Mikhailovna, "everyone else will be silent while Sasha Tiunova will sing on her own." At that her hands came down on the keys again.

The eyes of the representative lit up at this juncture somewhat. That was because Sasha Tiunova was singing. Now she had a really good voice.

In general she was a nice girl, Sasha Tiunova. I had been friends with her for a long time, ever since the time when she had paired up with me for walks. When we were taken out for walks we had to go along in pairs of course, holding each other by the hand. So it was Sasha that I used to hold by the hand and afterwards we became still better friends and always used to play and chat away together. Then some of the other children took into their heads to start teasing us. One of them I really gave what was coming to him and was properly told off after that of course by a teacher. To be on the safe side they made us change partners for walks: Sasha Tiunova was paired up with another boy and me with Zina Gvozdeva, a horrible snivelly little girl, who always had a runny nose that she used to wipe with the palm of her hand and then stretch out that same palm to me to take hold of when we went out for our walks.

But Sasha Tiunova and I still remained the best of friends.

I liked listening to her singing: she sang better than all the others, the other girls that is, because when it comes to the boys I sang best. Is that boasting? Well, and now. . . .

"And now," said Rosa Mikhailovna, "we shall sing the song about the merry geese and Zhenya Prokhorov will start us off."

I took a deep breath and waited for Rosa Mikhailovna to strike up before starting with the words:

Our Granny, she had two geese,
Two merry little geese . . .

Then everyone else took up the tune. For some reason everyone seemed in a terrible hurry, tripping over their words and fairly rattling along. This made Rosa Mikhailovna scamper over the keys as well.

Perhaps that song really should be sung at that speed, but for some reason I wanted to sing it slowly, lingering on those difficult vowels. I even modified the words a bit on purpose, so that those high, resonant vowels were repeated more than the song actually required. "Our Granny, she-ee-e had two ge-ee-ese. . . ."

The point was that I had a very high voice, even higher than Sasha Tiunova's. Perhaps a boy's voice has no business to be higher than a girl's but nothing can be done about it if that's the way things are, can they now?

"And now," said Rosa Mikhailovna, "our girls will do a Moldavian dance."

However all of a sudden the representative bent down to whisper something into the warden's ear. Vera Ivanovna replied, raising her eyebrows disapprovingly as she did so. But he went on to say something else, at which Vera Ivanovna merely shrugged her shoulders but eventually she stood up and announced in a constrained voice:

"We won't have the dance now, Rosa Mikhailovna. Children, you can all go out and play now, but you, Zhenya Prokhorov, stay behind."

With yelps of joy all the children made a beeline for the doors.

Now the only people that were left in the room were Vera Ivanovna, Rosa Mikhailovna, me and him—the representative who had really started throwing his weight around by then.

"Come over here," he said to me.

I walked over.

"So your name is Zhenya Prokhorov?"

"Yes."

"My name is Vladimir Konstantinovich," he

said by way of introduction, and then added his surname, "Namestnikov."

"Zhenya," the representative went on, "can you sing me something else?"

"Yes, I can," I replied. "I know every song."

"Every one?"

"Yes, every one."

I really did know a great many, because, as I said earlier, in our dormitory there was a wireless extension. I always used to listen to everything that billowed forth from the black loudspeaker. I quickly memorised all the songs that were broadcast, both the words and the music. Sometimes after I'd heard a song only once, or sometimes after a second hearing and definitely after a third repeat I would know a song from start to finish.

"Well, what are you going to sing then?"

On hearing that Rosa Mikhailovna blushed and said: "But, Vladimir Konstantinovich, I won't be able to accompany him, because I haven't got any music with me."

"Don't let that worry you," Vladimir Konstantinovich answered. "We can make do without. We'll manage won't we?..."

I moved back three steps then and nodded my head.

I sang him my favourite songs: "This is the fairest flower of all", "A little girl walks in the meadow", "The barges are bringing the mullet in".

While I was singing those songs Vladimir Konstantinovich both smiled and frowned but there were more smiles than frowns. All the time he listened hard.

"And now," I said awkwardly, "may I sing just one more song?"

"Of course," said Vladimir Konstantinovich with a nod.

"Which song?" asked Vera Ivanovna in a worried voice.

"The only thing is though, on the wireless it's not a man but a woman who sings the song." I felt embarrassed as I told him that. What was more I didn't know the whole song, just the opening lines. But I liked it very much.

"On you go," said Vladimir Konstantinovich.

I took another two steps backward. Then I forced down the lump that was stuck in my throat because as soon as I started thinking back to that song I started to feel sad. It was a rather sad song.

On that long-awaited day
We shall forget our plight.
Across the water far away
A ship will come into sight . . .

Whenever I used to listen to that song or sing it, I could always see quite clearly in my mind's eye the sea I had never set eyes on, the steam and the ship which I had never seen either, except in the cinema, and I used to imagine as well a very beautiful lady standing on the shore waiting, waiting till the ship appears. . . . And I used to think to myself that she would probably be waiting in vain.

As I said before, I didn't know the whole of the song, only the beginning. But I didn't have to sing any more of it, because I had hardly finished singing that first verse when Vladimir Konstantinovich suddenly took his spectacles off and brought a handkerchief out of his pocket to wipe his eyes: they had turned red and started to water. Probably the song had made him feel as sad as it used to make me.

"That's from 'Madame Butterfly'," said Rosa Mikhailovna to Vera Ivanovna.

Vera Ivanovna's eyes were benign again, she had calmed down by now. She had probably worried at the beginning that I would come out with something I had picked up in the street. But things didn't finish there.

"Well!" said Vladimir Konstantinovich in a merry voice putting his spectacles to rights on his nose. "Well now, Zhenya, come over here. . . ."

He went over to the piano and sat down on the revolving stool, which Rosa Mikhailovna quickly vacated for him. Oh, so that representative could play the piano! I had never seen representatives before who could play the piano!

"Zhenya, I am going to play a tune now and then I want you to clap out the rhythm for me."

He started playing and then I did my clapping.

He began playing again, another tune this time and I clapped away. There was nothing to it, it was simple. Pat-a-cake, pat-a-cake.

"That's fine," said Vladimir Konstantinovich. "Now I shall play a note and you sing it after me."

He played a note and I sang it after him. Then he played another, a higher one. I sang that one and then the next one still higher, and then higher.

"That's wrong," exclaimed Vladimir Konstantinovich all of a sudden, his eyes gleaming fiercely at me from behind his spectacles: "Quite wrong!"

"No, it isn't," I answered.

"Yes, it is!"

"But it isn't."

I wasn't in the least afraid of him though: people are not supposed to shout at us orphanage children. They can be had up for that, whatever kind of representatives they are!

"All right, I'll play it again," said Vladimir Konstantinovich. "Listen hard."

He played the note again. Then, all of a sudden, leaning over the keyboard, he started banging away fiercely at that black key. It looked as if he had got terrible angry, but it didn't seem to be me that he was angry with any more, for all of a sudden he swung right round on the stool, fixing his eyes on Rosa Mikhailovna and Vera Ivanovna.

"Would you be so kind as to tell me how many years ago you had the piano tuner here?"

"Well, you see, what with our tight budget . . ." Vera Ivanovna began. But then looking at me, she broke off in the middle and said: "Shall we let the boy go now?"

"Yes," answered Vladimir Konstantinovich.

"Off you go, Zhenya," said Vera Ivanovna.

By that time I had long been listening to the children shouting and calling to each other out in the yard. Things looked real fun out there, the other side of the window, not like it was in the hall.

"Good-bye," I said to Vladimir Konstantinovich, and then I ran out to join the others.

* * *

But late that evening, after we had all gone to bed and were curled up under the blankets, one of the nannies, Dunya, came running in, all flushed and out of breath: she was rather fat although she was young.

"Zhenya Prokhorov ... Vera Ivanovna wants to see you. Quick, hurry up!"

I had to get up and dress again.

Petka Zavarukha who was sleeping in the bunk above me—we all used to sleep in two-tier bunks —leant down and asked in a curious voice:

"What does she want you for? What have you gone and done?"

"I don't know...."

I really didn't know either. I hadn't done anything really bad; perhaps it was because I had been arguing cheekily with the representative?

It was dark in the corridor outside the 'dormitory, but there was yellow light shining out from underneath the warden's door which was slightly ajar. So I walked up to that door and stood there wondering whether I should go in or not. I heard a voice from inside saying:

"...a child's future. And I do not see any guarantee in what you've been telling me, no guarantee at all...." That was Vera Ivanovna's voice.

"There are no such things as hundred per cent guarantees." That was the representative's voice; so he hadn't gone home.

I went on standing there, listening to what they were saying, afraid to go in and not understanding a single word. I didn't know words like guarantee and per cent. If I didn't know them, how is it that I remembered them and am able to reproduce them now, a conversation I couldn't make head or tail of? Perhaps it sounds as if I'm fibbing, or inventing things? Perhaps I'm making up the whole intriguing story too? The part about the dog too? And the gramophone record? After all we orphanage children are accomplished inventors.

No. I'm not making any of it up. I'm not fibbing. I'm just relating things exactly as they happened.

However now that I'm nearly seventeen, of course there are some things that I have forgotten, things that have slipped my memory: it's impossible to remember every minute of one's past, everything you've ever said, or you've heard said, no one's memory can hold all that.

So I must confess from the beginning that that particular conversation which I listened to standing outside the door and others which were to take place later I shall be relating as I remember them looking back. The thing is though that I've learnt quite a bit since then and grown a little wiser.... Now I can imagine to myself quite clearly what I would have said, had I been in Vera Ivanovna's place. I can equally well imagine what I would have said in reply to the warden's arguments if I had been in Vladimir Konstantinovich Namestnikov's place.

"There are no such things as hundred per cent guarantees," he replied.

"Well, you know ..." sighed Vera Ivanovna. "It is possible to say quite confidently that he'd make a good locksmith or electrician, or perhaps eventually an engineer. But as for your line of country.... Vladimir Konstantinovich, I have been working in the teaching world for a long time and remember various cases among older pupils who saw themselves as Heaven knows what kind of celebrities or who had all sorts of ideas put into their heads; then they got carried away, forgot about everything else only to singe their wings in the end...."

"I don't deny that. More often than not that is what happens."

The legs of a chair scraped on the floor and I heard footsteps. The visitor had probably got up and started pacing up and down the warden's study.

"But you must realise, my dear Vera Ivanovna, you must understand that talent is such a rare thing! Probably the rarest thing on earth! To let it pass unnoticed, to lose it is criminal. Here on your very doorstep you've got a living wonder. . . ."

All of a sudden I felt very embarrassed. Although I was small, I knew quite well that eavesdropping was something to be ashamed of. So I knocked at the door and went in.

"Good evening," I said.

Vera Ivanovna was sitting at her desk, but Vladimir Konstantinovich came straight up to me and putting his hand on my shoulder said: "Zhenya, would you like to learn to sing properly?"

There was a fine idea for you. I even took offence.

"But can't I sing already?"

"No," he said. Then he repeated, "No, of course not!"

I looked at Vera Ivanovna in search of moral support in face of the terrible injustice. By this time though she was sitting there with her head bowed, not looking at me at all. It was as if she were deliberately avoiding my gaze.

"You are going to go to Moscow, where you will enter a music school," Vladimir Konstantinovich went on, still holding my shoulder in his firm grip. "You are going to sing in real choir, in Moscow. Thousand of boys want to join our choir. but. . . ."

He said something else as well but what came next I can't remember. I don't think I even heard what followed, I didn't think about anything else once I had heard the word "Moscow".

But no, something else did occur to me. I remembered to think of a few other matters and put forward a few conditions. I asked: "But what about Sasha Tiunova, is she going too? Are you going to take her along too?"

Vladimir Konstantinovich shook his head apologetically and said: "That's not possible. We only take boys at our school. It's a boys' choir."

So, that was that.

"And do your boys fight a lot?"

Vladimir Konstantinovich let go of my shoulder, wiped his wide forehead and with a sigh, replied: "Sometimes."

* * *

The first thing they did was to cut me off from all the others, the community I'd lived in for as long as I could remember.

The next morning Nanny Dunya took me by the hand and led me off to her house because it was she and no other who had been assigned the task of taking me to Moscow and she had to make the necessary preparations before we set off.

Nanny Dunya explained to me that I had to sit out a quarantine, that was what the professor had said. It turned out that the representative Vladimir Konstantinovich was a professor as well. When he had left he had given instructions that I must sit out a quarantine, although nobody was ill in the orphanage at that time. I wasn't ill either but what good was it arguing with a professor?

Nanny Dunya took me by the hand and, tucking a bundle under her other arm, led me off to her house. She lived at the very edge of the town in a delapidated little wooden house. I spent three whole days there, pining away. I was so bored, because right away I started missing my friends at the orphanage and, in general, life was much more fun at the orphanage than in the house where I now found myself.

Only once was the monotony broken.... Once when night was falling a visitor came to Dunya's house, a soldier complete with shoulder straps, a peaked cap and enormous boots. What was more it seemed to me that he was a little bit drunk: a strange new smell filled the room as soon as he came in and there was a bottle neck sticking out of his trouser pocket.

At first Nanny Dunya got very flustered when that soldier came and kept trying to push him out of the door before I caught sight of him. But the soldier didn't give up and protested loudly about being given such an unfriendly reception. Then Dunya herself lost her temper remonstrating with him in whispers, threatening that she would never let him near the house again. But when not even that threat had any effect on the undaunted soldier, Dunya pointed at me and pronounced the magic word "quarantine". At that he let up immediately, saluted, turned round and was gone.

The next day Dunya and I set off for the station, where there was a nice surprise waiting for me. In spite of the quarantine I was to be given a proper send-off. Vera Ivanovna herself had come and she had brought Sasha Tiunova with her: perhaps she had remembered that I had asked Professor Namestnikov if he would take her along to sing in the boys' choir.

Vera Ivanovna brought out a big box of sweets done up in ribbon from her bag and handed it to me. Then Sasha Tiunova brought out a handkerchief from her pocket with her own embroidery in the corner and all round the edges. "Here's a souvenir for you. I did the embroidery myself," she said.

"Good-bye, Zhenya," said Vera Ivanovna. "Remember to behave yourself and don't forget the collective you grew up in."

Then Dunya and I got into the railway carriage and talked to them out of the window: at last the train started pulling out and Vera Ivanovna, Sasha Tiunova, the station, the whole leafy town of Lipetsk that had been my home was swept away into the distance.

I had originally intended to spend the whole night looking out of the window, because it was the first time, as far as I could remember, that I had ever ridden on a train and had the chance to look out of the window and watch the world go by.

But it was already late and all there was to see out of the window was darkness apart from the occasional station lights. I felt sleepy and soon dropped off.

By morning we were already in Moscow.

* * *

What was it like?

To be honest to this day I still can't shake

 myself free of the first overwhelming impression which the capital made on me.

The thing that hit me was that Moscow was all underground.

Nanny Dunya and I had hardly got out of the train when we were caught up in a hectic whirl of people that swept us along. But where to? Nanny Dunya was clutching a piece of paper with the address of the place we had to go to on it, and shielding me from the surging crowd with their bulky cases that seemed deliberately to be trying to knock my head, she kept trying to stop someone to ask the way: "Please, mister, please, missus." But nobody responded to her appeal, nobody glanced at the piece of paper but merely pushed us further along in the direction everyone was going. However, it turned out later that that was just the answer we needed.

Only for a few minutes did the blue sky come into view but then it disappeared and we found ourselves in the Metro.

Here Nanny Dunya, who herself was in the city for the first time, again tried to make inquiries in relation to the address on the piece of paper merely to be pushed forward to the change counter, then to the turnstiles and then to a weird and wonderful staircase that takes you down a slope while you just stand there.

After we reached the bottom Nanny Dunya who was sweating and quite bewildered by this time turned to a man who was sitting there quite calmly reading his newspaper amidst all the hubbub to ask how we could get to Krasnopresnenskaya Station. "Which side of the platform do we need, mister?"

"Krasnopresnenskaya?" repeated the old fellow. "That side."

But no sooner had we moved off in the direction indicated when he called after us: "The other one will do just as well. It doesn't make any difference. It's a circle line."

"Drat you," muttered Dunya by way of a thank you as she pulled me over to the train.

After that we roared along underground for some time.

I was a little bit worried for I couldn't understand how the driver could find his way in such pitch dark, and was wondering uneasily what would happen if he took the wrong turning or lost his way down in the black maze and ended up in a place from where there'd be no way out. . . .

But every so often the train slowed down and we found ourselves in some brightly lit station. They were all like the one where we had got on and yet different because each one had its own special walls and type of decorations. People laden with shopping bags poured out in a thick stream only to have their places taken by another stream of people with more shopping bags.

Then off the train roared again in the darkness, only to slow down again before long and unload and load up again with lots of these people and their shopping.

I had the chance to ride along on the Metro to my heart's content during all the years that followed and was soon able to travel on it by myself quite independently, pick out the shortest route in the underground labyrinth from one point to the other and, like other people, I too came to appreciate the convenience and advantages of that form of transport, but nevertheless I could never shake off the impression that the Metro was what had come first and everything else had been built up on it as a pedestal or a marble foundation, all the Moscow that was above ground—the Kremlin, the Bolshoi, Novodevichy Convent, the Pushkin statue and the planetarium —but in the beginning was the Metro.

There was no need for Dunya to have got so flustered because everything turned out just as we had been told it would. The crowd had been right when it swept us along with it underground, the man with the newspaper had been right when he told us it didn't make any difference which side of the platform we got onto the train. That was soon borne out by the booming voice that resounded through the carriage announcing "Krasnopresnenskaya Station!"

That was where we had to get out. We went up the escalator and came out to find ourselves at a noisy crossroads. Cars were rushing past, trolley-buses whirred along and trams clanged by while militia-men blew their whistles and pedestrians scurried to and fro.

So this was Moscow?! I took a look around . . . and gaped in amazement.

Behind the Metro station loomed a mountain of stone. It was recklessly high and the pinnacles that soared skywards made it seem even higher than it actually was. What was more it was an enormous sprawling mountain complete with foothills, ridges and spurs. And to think that this mountain housed people! Windows, windows, so many you couldn't possibly count them. You could probably have fitted the whole of Lipetsk into that mountain!

When I started to compare the height of the mountain with the depth of the Metro we had just come out of, my head started spinning and I clutched Dunya's hand.

"Oh, you poor little chap!" she exclaimed. "To think you haven't eaten anything the whole morning, you've had no breakfast. This Moscow's enough to make anyone go daft!"

We were lucky though, for right there, under our very noses there was a woman selling pies. Dunya bought some that were all hot, sticky and golden brown. They were so delicious that we gobbled them all down on the spot and licked our lips afterwards. Moscow pasties turned out to be quite heavenly!

After that we didn't have much difficulty in finding the address we were looking for: 4/6, Bolshaya Gruzinskaya Street. There were leafy poplars growing behind the railings which almost hid from view the old two-storeyed building.

Later I shall say more about that building where I was to spend the next ten years of my life. But not now. . . .

The next thing that happened was that we were told it was not the building we needed, that this beautiful old house was where the boys had their lessons and that they lived some distance away in Krasnaya Presnya district.

My long-awaited arrival was duly noted down in some book or other and we were told to get going for the new destination. Get going we did.

Thank Heavens it turned out to be quite near. We walked past the courtyard of a shabby building looking for the back entrance (we had been expressly told to use the back entrance). It was so dark we were hard put to it to find our way, but at last we got up onto the first floor, opened a door and found ourselves in a corridor with walls painted in some dingy emulsion.

An old woman in a blue overall appeared from somewhere—she must have been a cleaning woman or a matron—and inquired in a matter-of-fact voice: "New boy?"

"Yes, he's new," replied Dunya. "I've brought him along."

"Well, now," said the old woman, with a sigh. "What's his name?"

"Zhenya. He's a good boy, our Zhenya. Does what he's told."

"All our boys here are good boys," the old woman went on and picking up the mop that was leaning against the wall, repeated: "All of them do what they're told."

"May I ..." Dunya began timidly. "May I have a peep at the room he'll be in, the place where he'll sleep?"

"All right, have a look. There's the door over there."

Dunya and I went over to the door that had been pointed out to us and opened it a crack.

"Golly!" gasped Dunya quite dumbfounded.

Behind that door was a room more enormous than anything I had ever seen. Yet despite its huge size it looked very cramped because it was crammed full from end to end with iron beds. There must have been a hundred at least (I admitted at the beginning that I couldn't count further than a hundred in those days and whenever there was a lot of something I made it a hundred). There they were—a hundred, identical, tidily made beds. But they were all empty, there wasn't a soul in the enormous whole room. But no, there in a distant corner could be seen someone's head and feet.

"Golly," said Dunya again, "why, its worse than our ..." but then she covered her mouth with her hand and so I never knew what she had meant to say.

"Well, come on, my girl, say your good-byes to the lad," commanded the old woman. "Outsiders aren't meant to hang around for long in here."

"I'm not an outsider," protested Dunya and started to cry. "But the poor little scrap's going to be left all by himself."

"All by himself! A fat chance there is of that here! There's a whole army of them. When they all come pouring in . . . it's all hell let loose. And outsiders aren't allowed to linger around for long."

So there was nothing we could do but say good-bye.

When she said good-bye, Nanny Dunya took out of her bag the big box of sweets that Vera Ivanovna had brought to the station and then on the quiet so that nobody should see, she slipped a five-ruble note into my pocket.

3

"What's your name?"

I told him.

"What's you surname?"

I told him.

"Where are you from?"

I let on.

"Well then. Come over here, Prokhorov."

I went over.

"Pleased to meet you." At that he stretched out two fingers for me to shake. He was lying on his bed on top of the covers with his legs crossed and what's more with his shoes on.

I said before that when Dunya and I had peeped into the room that was to be mine I had caught sight of somebody's head and feet in the opposite corner of the room. Well, on closer inspection it turned out that that head and those feet belonged to two different owners. The head belonged to a boy who was sitting on the bed, a very small, swarthy boy with very dark eyes, who seemed very frightened and who looked as if he was a new boy like me, too. The feet belonged to the boy who was lying on the bed with his shoes on. He was a great hulk of a fellow! He had a head too of course. His face was broad with prominent cheek-bones and his enormous ears stuck out at right angles so that his face was a good deal wider than it was long. And when he started to grin, well! . . .

"What's that you're carrying under your arm, Prokhorov?"

"Sweets," I replied.

"Ah! Sweets. Chocolates, I suppose?"

With one bound the Hulk was on his feet, his eyes almost popping out of his head.

"Are you not aware, young man, that chocolate is bad for the vocal chords? What have you come here for, to study singing or to eat chocolate?"

I just wanted to sink through the floor. . . .

"Hand over that filth!"

I handed him the box and he hurried to undo the string, then opened the box, thrust his fist inside and stuffed a whole handful of chocolates into his cavern of a mouth all at one go.

His jaw bones started to work away and he squidged up his eyes like a cat starting to purr, while his fingers went on routing round the box.

"And what's that here? A bottle? With a liqueur in it? Where were you dragged up?!"

With a hearty munch he broke open the chocolate bottle and swallowed it down. A few moments later all that was left in the box were a few insipid looking sweets, which he had probably only left because he had no room for any more. The Hulk pushed the box away and said: "Help yourselves . . . but make sure this is the last time!"

Then he lay back on the pillows again, stretched out his legs and started to stroke his tummy.

"Marat," he addressed the dark-eyed boy in a quiet voice, sounding rather sorry for himself, "bring us a glass of water. You'll find a tap out in the corridor. There's a glass there as well."

Marat walked obediently over to the door.

"And what's your name?" I asked, plucking up my courage, because so far only I had introduced myself.

"Nikolai Ivanovich Biryukov, but you can call me Nikolai Ivanovich."

"What form are you in?" I then made so bold as to ask.

"Form IV," the Hulk replied. "I've just gone up into Form IV."

At that time I wasn't surprised by that piece of information, it didn't appear strange or even funny that the Hulk who referred to himself as Nikolai Ivanovich turned out to be only in Form IV and therefore a mere three years older than me. Now I would have laughed of course, but in those days things were quite different. A difference like that only appears unimportant to adults and those who almost belong to that category. But for children it is an important glaring difference. A pupil from Form II looks upon any first-former as small fry, a mere nobody, while a first-former sees a pupil from Form IV as an enormous all-powerful giant who is either a threatening bully or someone you can rely on to stick up for you.

At that stage I didn't know which of the two he was going to be for me, this Hulk with the face as broad as it was long, who had eaten up all my sweets.

"And you . . . do you sing as well?" I asked.

"Wha-a-at?"

Nikolai Ivanovich Biryukov jumped up from the bed once more with his eyes popping out of his head again.

"What was that you said? 'As well'! You should ask who else sings here other than Nikolai Ivanovich Biryukov. Nikolai Biryukov is leading treble, the choir's principal soloist! When Biryukov hits top A flat. . . ." He stood up straight, took a deep breath, opened his mouth and . . . a perfectly hideous, ear-splitting sound rent the air.

I shuddered, yet realised that the horrible squawk had not come from Nikolai Biryukov's throat but from outside the window that was wide open.

"Who's that?"

"That?" Biryukov rushed over to the window and leant out over the sill. "That's a pink flamingo."

"A pink what?" I said in astonishment and also started to clamber up on the window-sill.

"Flamingo," came the answer.

"How?"

"D'you mean to say you don't know! We're next to the Zoo."

He helped me up and there below the window no more than a hundred paces away was a concrete wall, and a thick row of trees through which there peeped a shining strip of blue water. From this perch I could also see that all across the mirror of the pond's surface were birds swimming leisurely to and fro, singly and in groups. White ones, black ones, blue ones, green ones and pink ones. They were bobbing up and down in the water, flapping their wings, squawking, squeaking, croaking, hissing and then again that piercing sound drowned all that hullabaloo. . . .

"There goes the pink flamingo," repeated my neighbour in tones of admiration. "What a bird!"

"I've never been to the Zoo."

"Never at all?"

"Never."

"What about dough?"

"Dough? . . . Aha," I said at last catching on and brought out the five-ruble note which Dunya had given me. "I've got some."

"What are we waiting for then?" exclaimed Nikolai Ivanovich leaping to his feet. He took the note from my hand, gave me a suspicious look and asked: "Where d'you get the lolly?"

"The matron gave it to me. Nanny Dunya."

"Well done, Nanny! Well done, Dunya!" said Nikolai Ivanovich happily.

"We are going to the Zoo," he announced in a final tone. "Children love the animals, who are our ancestors!"

The door opened and in came Marat carrying a tumbler, trying not to spill the water in it as he went, screwing up his dark eyes in concentration.

"Much obliged," acknowledged Nikolai Ivanovich and throwing back his head polished off the water at one gulp. Then he pulled the collar of Marat's shirt away from his neck and sprinkled the remaining drops down his back.

* * *

The next three hours we spent wandering round the Zoo.

We saw elephants, a big one and a baby one. We saw polar bears, down a deep pit inside a concrete enclosure with iron spikes jutting up round the top of it; one of them was diving around in a little lake blowing out water and snorting whenever he surfaced while the other was playing on the bank squeezing and gnawing away at an old car tyre. Then we saw a hippopotamus, not the whole of it though, only its eyes, which stuck up above the water while the rest of the hippopotamus was hidden under water and he refused to come out however much people called him and despite all the rolls and buns that they threw down for him. We saw a striped tiger and a striped zebra, a spotted leopard and a kangaroo with a great big tail, a crocodile pretending to be a log and a highly talkative parrot.

It was the first time I had ever seen all those wild animals, but Nikolai Ivanovich led me round from cage to cage with the confident air of an old hand. There was no end to the crowds at the Zoo. Above all it was full of children because it was the last day of the summer holidays and for lots of people, just as it was for me, it was the last day before they were to go to school for the very first time.

Yet we managed to find a corner of the Zoo

where there were hardly any people. At any rate no one lingered there very long even if they did appear. They just walked past without showing any interest, for behind the bars in this part of the Zoo there weren't any rare and wonderful beasts brought to Moscow from hot or cold countries far, far away. There were just an ordinary hare, an ordinary fox and an ordinary wolf.

They all seemed to be in a bad mood, running round their cages in circles as if they were desperate to get out, looking out from their plank pens with wistful eyes, as if they were trying to say: what have we been brought here for? The elephant, well that's clear, the same goes for the hippopotamus and the giraffe too, its neck by itself is worth coming to have a look at! We ourselves had never seen freaks like that before . . . but why us? We're no strangers, we're locals, you can see us in the woods, why go and put us in cages? They've even gone and put an elk behind bars, and a silly old billy-goat. . . . You people, you! . . .

There was a glum-looking wolf running from one side to the other of his cage of iron bars. Then after tiring himself out he lay down resting his head on his paws.

"Just like a dog," I said.

"He is a dog," said Nikolai Ivanovich. "It's a great big lie to say they're vicious, they're not vicious at all. They never attack people without being attacked themselves first. People go and attack them first, for money, because there is a good reward attached. But then people can get paid for dogs too, for rounding them up off the streets."

"My life was saved by a dog," I said.

"What d'you mean saved?"

I explained briefly how my life had been saved by an Alsatian and while I was telling the story I watched Nikolai Ivanovich closely, wondering whether he would believe my story or think I had invented it all. However Nikolai Ivanovich listened attentively and sympathetically and as far as I could see he believed every word of my story and nodded when I'd finished.

In general I'd noticed that now, out there in the Zoo by the cages with the wild and the ordinary animals, Nikolai Ivanovich little resembled the brash, merciless Hulk I'd come across in the hostel, who had eaten up all my sweets and poured water down Marat's collar. I even thought to myself that if I were to pluck up my courage it might be quite easy to address him as just plain Kolya instead of Nikolai Ivanovich.

"Let's go and look at the monkeys," proposed Kolya.

So, off we went to the monkeys. The crowd at the monkey-house was quite indescribable. The cages were besieged. Grown-ups were climbing on top of each other and children were pushing through their legs.

Kolya Biryukov came running up to the crowd, bent his head down and cut into the sea of people. I went after him and we managed to squeeze our way through, only to be pushed in different directions so that I soon lost sight of my companion. For all that though I had got as far as the actual wire-netting and there behind it the monkeys were playing the fool.

They were hanging by their tails, rocking to and fro on swings and chasing each other. Some of them were having a cuddle and others were fighting. They were scratching their tummies, scratching the napes of their necks as if they were working out new ways of attracting people's attention. One oldish monkey was holding a teeny-weeny one on its knees and painstakingly inspecting its fur, picking out the fleas and executing them. Another mother had caught hold of her offspring who had run wild and was giving him a hiding for all he was worth.

The onlookers were laughing fit to burst. I was killing myself too.

Perhaps all the capers the monkeys were up to then were just part of their ordinary everyday monkey life, yet it seemed to me that the monkeys were going out of their way to amuse and divert the onlookers. It was as if they were really pleased to see so many people all gathered round their particular cages—their crowd was bigger than any other in the whole Zoo—to know that here people were treading on each other's feet, having their buttons torn off and splitting their sides all the same, laughing till they cried.

I spent at least an hour watching the monkeys and would have been only too happy to spend another hour as well. But by that time I was getting worried because there had been no sign of Kolya Biryukov for a good long time. I thought to myself that perhaps it wasn't so interesting for Kolya to watch those monkeys as it was for me; after all he'd been there lots of times and I had never seen them before.

I wormed my way out of the crowd after just as long a struggle as the one I had had before to get through to the cage.

I looked round but there was no sign of Kolya. So that meant he must still be in there by the cage and I ought to wait for him. I sat down on a bench ... it was a long sit. People who had had their fill of watching the monkeys and laughing at their antics moved away from the monkey-house but there was always another lot to take their place. There was no sign of Nikolai Ivanovich though.

I waited a bit longer but there was still no sign of him. In the end I realised that there was probably no point in waiting for him. He in his turn had probably waited and waited for me and then got up and gone, thinking that I'd got lost.

I was only seven and it was my first day in an unfamiliar town, in Moscow. On my first day I had gone and lost myself and got stranded. Sitting on my bench I started to sob bitterly.

Did I say sob? Not on your life! If anyone thought I just sat down and sobbed they'd be very much mistaken. He wouldn't know much about us orphanage children, if he thought something like that. That's not the kind of thing we, "poor orphans", go in for. We're an independent lot and we never lose our heads wherever we happen to find ourselves. That's the last thing we would do!

I wiped the tears away with the back of my hand and got up from the bench. Over the green tops of the trees I could just see the crown of the building I'd gaped at in the morning—the one like a mountain. Through the Zoo railings I could also see the old two-storey building where Dunya and I had gone to announce my arrival that morning. So if I went out into the street, walked straight along and then took a side turning I was bound to come to the hostel.

I strode over to the exit. By the gate there was a stall where a woman was selling ice-cream. How wonderful it was in Moscow the way everything was on hand just when you wanted it. I gathered up the crumpled rubles and the small change that was left over after we had bought the tickets for the Zoo and bought myself an eskimo-pie: I turned back the silver paper, bit into the chocolate at the top and licked the cold ice-cream inside. Scrumptious!

I ambled along the street tucking into my ice-cream, licking up the melted bits that were starting to run down and slide away first on one side and then on the other.

All of a sudden I bumped into somebody's tummy that was barring the way, into someone's grey jacket, that higher up sported a blue tie with spots and to one side a leather document case tucked under an arm.

Then I saw his round spectacles pinned on me from above.

It was him. The representative. Vladimir Konstantinovich Namestnikov.

I was about to say "Good afternoon" to him, tell him it was me, that I'd been brought here as he'd instructed. But then I took fright at the thought that he would ask me how I came to be in this street, what I was doing roaming about by myself and why I had left the hostel without permission ... so I didn't say anything.

He didn't say anything either at first, just took the half-finished eskimo-pie out of my hand. So that was it, I might have known. Now he would stick it straight into his mouth as the Hulk in the hostel had done with my sweets and then send me for a glass of water. Was that really all they had brought me to Moscow for, to have people pinch every single thing I had one after the other?

Vladimir Konstantinovich looked round, walked up to a litter bin and with a look of disgust on his face threw my eskimo-pie away into it. As he came back he wiped his fingers carefully on a handkerchief, and then bent down to me and said: "Remember, that's the last ice-cream you're ever going to eat."

4

That was how my life at school began.

Early in the morning after we had woken up, washed and dressed, we set off from the hostel to the school, from Krasnaya Presnya Street to Bolshaya Gruzinskaya Street. We went on foot of course because it's not all that far although when the autumn months had passed and winter began that morning walk was not the most pleasant of pastimes. It wasn't so much the actual cold, although it was often bitter enough to make us run all the way to the school, or the wind that blew in our faces, or the slippery pavements, they were all mere trifles. The really unpleasant thing about it was that we had to set out when it was still dark. It was like darkest night in the street at that hour when with our coat-collars turned up and the ear-flaps of our winter caps pulled well down we trotted along from Presnya to Gruzinskaya Street. Of course there were street lamps and lighted windows in the houses, the yellow gleam of the passing trams and rear lights of cars glowing red like smouldering coals, and the green lights twinkling on the wind-screens of taxis for hire. The streets were also full of people hurrying to work, seething and streaming towards the Metro—the real day had begun, there was no mistaking it.

But you had only to lift your gaze, or look out

of the corner of your eye to see that the sky was still full of night, thick, sleepy, impenetrable.... Your lips would part to let out a warm little yawn only to be transformed into a cloud of cold steam.

But almost before you noticed it you were inside the school door and the cloakroom was under siege. Our noses would give a sensitive twitch and instantly define the smells rising aloft from the dining hall.

"Is it meat rissoles?"

"Yes."

"Lads, it's meat rissoles."

To this day I have no idea of the scientific explanation for the link between our senses of smell and hearing. However I personally am convinced that there definitely is such a link: for instance in our school they take in boys with perfect pitch, in other words who have good voices and a faultless ear for music. Yet both I and all my new friends, including the enemies among them, every single person in the school in fact possessed in addition to this perfect ear for music an astonishing sense of smell—they always knew what was being prepared down in the basement kitchen for breakfast, dinner or supper. Two floors away we could tell just as infallibly goulash and macaroni from goulash and mashed potatoes, as we could tell double top G from double top G flat.

When drop scones were being cooked, which was a fairly frequent happening, no really sharp sense of smell was required: eyes were enough, for as soon as we crossed the threshold our eyes started to water. All the floors, all the corridors and all the classrooms were full of acrid, slightly bitter grey smoke, which lingered around for ages. It was particularly overpowering at the sacred hour in our early morning routine, when our early choir practice was in progress. That smoke used to penetrate the room where we were singing and stop there for a long time, making our throats tickle.

But more of those choir practices later. . . . First of all I'll dwell on the other lessons, namely the subjects that are taught in any school, the bedrock of any education.

We were taught the three R's—ma-ma, pa-pa; down stroke thick, up stroke thin; two and two make four.

Normally there wouldn't be any need to mention all that—that's something everyone's familiar with, it's something everyone has had to go through. Yet in our case there was one important difference. . . .

In all ordinary schools people are taught to write first using three lines with diagonals to keep the letters even, then two lines with diagonals, then you drop the diagonals and eventually advance to a single line. After that you can write any way you please.

We didn't start off like that though. We began neither with three nor two lines but five, five lines drawn with white chalk across the blackboard. Every class from the bottom of the school to the top had an identical board on which were ruled several staves.

Notes were drawn in on those rows of lines, first of all by the teacher—C,D,E,F,G,A,B,C—treble and bass clefs, crotchets and quavers, sharps and flats. But soon we too were able to write them in on those blackboards and at our sight-reading lessons we used to sing all that we had written up on the board. We were even taught to conduct, in 3/4 time, 4/4 time and any old time under the sun.

But, as I said before, music was not the only thing we were taught. There was arithmetic and there was writing and all the usual subjects.... But the boards, the blackboards in every classroom had sets of five-line staff notations ruled across them.

That was why we wrote our first ever A's and B's in chalk fitting them into five lines, sticking out our tongues from the strain. We also learnt our two-times table with the help of those same five lines. During break-time we used to draw all kinds of funny faces in those same staves.

There was no choice because the blackboards were nailed to the walls for keeps with great big nails and no one's going to start taking down the board and fixing up another one in its place before every lesson!

Moreover, it seems to me that there was something else behind all that business about the boards, not a scheme deliberately devised by someone but a special significance all the same.

We were taught the three R's in our school, as in all others, by one and the same teacher. She was a kind old woman with grey hair called Ksenia Vassilyevna, and I'm sure it's as it should be that small children should have one and the same teacher for those subjects when they first start school, otherwise they would get muddled over who was teaching them what. What's more, who would they be referring to when with tears in their eyes they sang the song "My first teacher" on their farewell evening before they left school.

I for one don't know who we'll be addressing that song to, for when I started school our class did not just have Ksenia Vassilyevna but half a dozen other teachers as well; for scales, piano, music theory, choir. All Ksenia Vassilyevna had to do was see that we could read, write and do sums.

Music came first. Like the staves ruled on all the boards it was always just under the surface. It never let you forget it was just round the corner and that Music was at the base of everything, above everything, the most important thing in the world. Please note!!

* * *

We were well aware of that already though.

Each morning started off with singing practice. First lesson was always choir practice. We assembled in a small hall, where there was a piano and where music-stands had been put out. We took our places behind the music-stands, trebles on the right, altos on the left. Even before the choir-master appeared we used to start shushing away. I must confess that the first day or two I found it very strange and even funny: they'd promised that we'd be taught to sing and instead of that—sh-sh-sh.

Soon however I was to discover the point of all the shushing. It turned out that the most important thing for the singer to learn was how to breathe properly, to control his breathing. You fill your chest with air and then gradually, bit by bit, very slowly, as slowly as you possibly can, you let it out again through your mouth. If you don't learn how to do that correctly, you'll never be able to sing anything properly, because you'll waste all your breath on the first few notes and start suffocating in the middle of a word and gasping for air like a fish that's been dragged out of the water.

Later I was to hear all sorts of fantastic stories about the art of breath control; how in olden times singers were made to sing with a lighted candle right in front of their faces, without making the flame give the slightest quiver, as if they weren't breathing at it. Was that just a conjurer's trick, nonsense, tomfoolery? No, there was no tomfoolery about it. There really have been singers like that who were able to hold one loud and powerful note for a whole minute at a stretch—a whole minute. Sometimes ice-hockey players can score three goals in a single minute and a singer can keep on going, keep on singing for all that time on one and the same breath, just one. . . .

Those were singers, those were!

Well, we were trained to do the same kind of thing too. We filled our lungs with air and gently blew it out again, letting it escape through our teeth. But why the shushing sound? There was no real need for it of course. It was just that small boys of that age as a rule are short of teeth; our milk teeth were in the process of falling out one by one and everyone was bound to have the odd gap. It was the gaps that made us shush as we let the air out. A hundred mouths, there's a hundred gaps for you, a regular steam engine—sh-sh-sh-sh-sh-sh.

Then in would come Vladimir Konstantinovich Namestnikov.

He greeted us, gave a nod to Sergei Pavlovich at the piano and off we went.

"Fokin, open your throat. . . ."
"Petrov, fill your lungs!"
"More tone! Rounder on those top notes!"
"Makaveyev, breathe from lower down!"
"Think about what you're singing?"

And all that was while we were just doing scales and exercises. But at first I didn't sing, I just stood there listening. We new boys were told just to be there, but not take part.

"She sells sea-shells sitting on the sea-shore."
"Faster!"
"She sells sea-shells sitting on the sea-shore."
"Now the thrushes."
"Thirty-three thrushes flew through the thrubbery."

Everybody burst out laughing and we new boys also joined in the peals of laughter. Next to me stood Marat, my class-mate, who was also laughing. Now he should have been the last person to laugh: how was he going to fare later on when we in our turn would also be made to rattle off those tongue-twisters to improve our enunciation? For when all was said and done, dark-eyed Marat Aliev from the Caucasus standing next to me didn't find even talking Russian all that easy.

"Haydn's 'Advent of Spring'."

I felt a thrill of excitement in anticipation of what was to come. It was not the first time I had heard that song all about spring coming; it was not so much the words about spring that excited me, particularly seeing that outside it was still the depths of winter, but the thought that by the spring I should most probably be singing that song along with the others, I should be allowed to sing in the choir—the sooner the better!

However, my excitement was not really due to the thought of the spring to follow, nor to the fact that I would be singing with the others by then, I was looking forward to the song for its own sake.

The boys spread out their copies on their music-stands, but Sergei Pavlovich, the man sitting at the piano, put his music away. He didn't need it, for there was not going to be any piano accompaniment this time. There would be just the boys' voices. Now I know that such unaccompanied music is termed *a capella.*

A hundred clear voices soar aloft to the skies, not just to the dark ceiling of the small practice-room but to the bright blue sky outside, like a flock of birds, not just one flock but four because the choir was singing in four parts. The parts did not merge together in a single flow of sound but interwove with each other, as the voices drew apart and came together again. And each of those four parts in its turn was made up of individual boys' voices that together produced a single pure note. Yet all of a sudden I thought I could pick out the most tuneful line of all in that pure sound and looking round whom should I find but Nikolai Ivanovich Biryukov, singing away with his mouth wide open. . . .

"Spring is here, all ye birds! Spring is here, all ye brothers. Hearken, spring is here!"

Then all of a sudden I felt my ears twinge. I almost lost my balance. Then I noticed that Vladimir Konstantinovich himself looked a bit shaky on his pins.

The choir went on singing in a disciplined way, but then the conductor stretched out his hand to interrupt the singing.

Namestnikov turned round towards the window; a car had just hooted outside. Just under that window was a parking place for cars: we had very important neighbours, we overlooked the Ministry of Geology and the chauffeurs sometimes used to get impatient waiting for their overdue passengers.

Vladimir Konstantinovich was looking over towards the open fanlight. He must have been wondering whether it should be shut or not. Suppose again just at the most inopportune moment ... but on the other hand the fanlight couldn't possibly be closed, since the hall was so horribly cramped. That hall where we had our choir practice every morning was really tiny and inside there were a hundred voices at work—a hundred mouths, a hundred pairs of lungs hungry for air. Sometimes there just wasn't enough for everybody. Sometimes it would get to the pitch where we just couldn't sing any more and occasionally one of us might come over faint....

No, the fanlight couldn't possibly be closed.

Vladimir Konstantinovich turned back to the choir again and said in a stern, annoyed voice: "No, this is no way to work, my friends! To W-O-R-K.... This part won't do at all." He then proceeded to sing a passage falsetto. "We'll sing each part separately, starting with the altos. Trebles wait for the time being.... Now, concentrate!"

This time there were no longer four flocks of birds soaring aloft but only two, the ones that had been flying lower down. It wasn't the same thing at all: not the same music, not the same spring, not the same Haydn.

That was the way we did things.

The altos sang away, while the trebles waited.

It was all right for the altos but not for the trebles who could hear how the high voices were missing, which at this point when the altos fall away sharply, would have swept heavenwards!

All at once someone standing near me couldn't hold out any more and I heard him start humming softly under his breath. Then another timid voice started up. . . .

"Stop! What's going on? I said the trebles were to wait. It looks as if someone wants to leave choir practice?"

Not a word was to be heard after that. No one wanted to leave the room. It was just that the trebles wanted to sing, when they weren't supposed to, when it was the altos' turn.

We new boys also wanted to sing with all the rest, but our time had not yet come.

5

That was how we lived—surrounded by music, all day and every day. Of course there were lots of other things as well, that I'll talk about later when the time comes: about love, about crooks, about playing truant, about searching for hidden treasure. Yes, all sorts of things happened, but all in good time.

It's music's turn now though. I must talk about it, although that's a very difficult undertaking, or rather a completely impossible one.

To talk about music or try to describe it—well you just can't. It has a language of its own, which can't be translated into any other. And there's nothing you can do to change that.

If it was just me, who found it impossible to

 talk about music and describe it! . . . But who can?

Take the great musician Alexander Scriabin for instance, perhaps the greatest of all great musicians. At any rate for me he is just that. All his life he tried to describe his music to other people and convey its essence in words. Each time he wrote a symphony he immediately put out a book to explain it all, saying what he was trying to do where. He even taught himself to write verse so as to be able to paraphrase his music in verse form. Yet verse remains verse and cannot take the place of music, and they have nothing really in common.

It is not purely by chance that I mentioned Alexander Scriabin at this stage. Almost as soon as I had joined the music school, during that first winter we were taken to hear a concert in the Grand Hall of the Conservatoire. Now, several years later, I find it strange that they took us new boys to hear Scriabin: the senior boys, well, that would have been understandable, not even Scriabin could have amazed them, they would not have been out of their depth . . . but as for us first-formers. . . . At that time we were hardly able to read music and manoeuvring our fingers as we went we could just about manage the inevitable "Twinkle, twinkle, little star. . ."—and then out of the blue, Scriabin!

Yet when I start to think about it I realise now that it was not really bad teaching tactics. After all, the best way to teach children how to swim is to throw them in the deep end and let them get on with it as best they can.

To get back where I started, let me repeat, we were taken to hear Scriabin. All the boys at the school, the whole choir, turned up in the Grand

Hall and we took our seats in a most orderly and demure fashion.

The concert hall was indeed grand and most imposing. It was snow-white from end to end and all down each side hung portraits of famous composers: one with a beard, another with moustaches, a third with grey hair, a fourth with a windswept mane. On that occasion I did not know any of them by sight yet, but just sensed that they were famous.

There were lots of musicians on the stage, at least a hundred: all of a sudden they started playing their instruments, each one blowing or scraping away what he pleased, not paying the slightest attention to what his neighbour was doing. They must have forgotten to tune their fiddles and pipes and now be hastily making up for lost time in front of all the audience. What a noise it made, enough to send you clean out of your mind!

At last it all quietened down. Then a lady came forward, her high heels clicking as she walked, and announced: "Scriabin's 'Poem of Ecstasy'", and then walked away with the same stately air.

Her appearance was followed by the impetuous entrance, almost at a run, of a man in a black jacket which was split down the middle at the back to give it two tails and a dazzling white shirt and a tie that was every bit as white.

That made the audience immediately start clapping, although it seemed to me that it was still early to applaud, for after all the man hadn't done anything special to deserve it all, apart from getting up on to the cupboard in the middle of the stage with a jump that looked very nimble for his age.

The conductor raised his stick and silence fell. I didn't even notice when the music started, it was so soft. It was so soft that you couldn't possibly tell where the silence stopped and the music began. I was surprised that they'd collected so many people up there on the stage to play such soft music, three people counting the conductor would have been quite enough. I started to feel bored and look around me.

I soon discovered that I was not the only person who was feeling bored. In the next row there was a little frail old man who had folded his hands on his stomach and half closed his eyes: it looked as if he had fallen asleep. There was a funny old man for you! He could have had a nap at home and yet he'd come all the way to a concert for it.

Then I looked to the other side of me. On the right there was some fellow holding a thick book, whose pages were crammed full of notes, that he was reading most attentively; he kept turning the pages and every now and then he looked up at the conductor, then he would start reading again and I could have sworn that he was making sure with the help of that book that the musicians were playing correctly and that the conductor was waving his stick properly, to see that everything was as it should be. What sticklers some people are! A fat woman in a dress with a lace collar noticed that I was looking round and wagged a discreet warning finger at me.

After that I looked straight ahead of me. I was lucky though, I couldn't have asked for more: to save me from getting hopelessly bored there was a bald man sitting right in front of me. He was quite bald, without a single hair on his head and over that head of his a moth was circling. It was an ordinary moth, like the kind that always fly round woollen clothes. What could the silly old moth be looking for on that man's bald head, what was it planning to scrounge when there was nothing, not a single thing there? As if it had read my thoughts, the moth flew disappointedly away.

It was only then that I noticed that the orchestra had started to play a good deal louder. The violinists were plying their bows to and fro, and the trumpeters' cheeks were puffed out, while the drummer was bent over his drum.

I tried to concentrate, for after all I had been brought here to listen to a concert, not to look around me. I should be listening, picking out some tune I suppose: after all I had made a habit of picking up tunes at first hearing ever since I had been very small and then trying them out on the orphanage piano. Well why not try and do the same thing here as well. I pricked up my ears. But I couldn't find any tune, I couldn't pick one out from among the thick web of voices and sounds—no matter how hard I tried.

But then I did catch the boldest of the trumpets, that set itself apart from the rest of the orchestra and played something all of its own: "Ta-tu-um, ta-tu-um, ta-tu-um", up high and then "ta-ta-ta-ta-ta" lower down: then more insistent still—"ta-tu-um, ta-tu-um!"

But could you call that a tune? What on earth kind of tune was it! Just try and remember it, you'd never be able to.

That reminded me I had been told by the older boys that if you show a trumpeter a lemon while he is playing his trumpet—even from a distance —he has to stop playing because his cheeks start to contract at once at the sight of that sour fruit.

 That would have been something really worth trying out, if only I had had a lemon with me. . . .

Meanwhile the flurry in the orchestra grew apace. More and more voices started joining in the general medley and sometimes the collision of those voices was so startling that I shuddered.

The conductor was waving his hands about in a frenzy by this time, leaning over first to one side and then to the other. But just then something else made me forget the music. I noticed a drop on the conductor's nose.

You see I was sitting fairly near the stage and a bit to one side. This gave me a clear view of a drop on the end of the conductor's nose. It was hanging on the very end of his nose. Perhaps it was a drop of sweat that had run down from his forehead, after all he was waving his arms about very wildly, work like that was enough to make anyone break out into a sweat. Or perhaps he just had a cold, for it was winter and he could have caught a cold on his way to the concert.

Probably the conductor himself could feel that there was a drop hanging on the end of his nose and would have liked to get rid of it, to shake it off. But he hadn't got a chance. All the musicians were watching their music with one eye and with the other they were carefully following every movement the conductor made. Even if he tried to touch his nose on the sly it would be enough to bewilder the orchestra and make everyone lose their place and then they'd all be done for.

Then there came another quiet patch, only short little gasping sighs reminded you now of what had been going on a few moments before: I could feel even by my own breathing how difficult it was to get your breath back after such wild playing.

The resounding trumpet that had been drowning the whole of the orchestra had faded away into the distance somewhere; yet it seemed to me as if the echo of its insistent, compelling call was still hovering in the midst of the restful calm that had since set in.

But the calm didn't last for long. It all started up again with renewed vigour. Not one of the hundred musicians was sitting idle now: I hardly had time to glance from the violins to the flutes, from the 'cellos to some wooden pipes or other standing upright on the stage. They were all being played at once and all of a sudden I felt worried that I wouldn't be able to find my bearings in that maze of sounds, among those groaning, ringing, shouting monsters.

Not my eyes but my ears led me to an enormous swirling boa-constrictor of a trumpet, that all of a sudden let forth a wild cry from its gaping jaws. Then the sound sank lower and lower into the bowels of the earth until all at once it ceased to be a whole sound, scattering itself as it were in separate little shivers, each one making your ear-drums tingle as it reached you.

I sat there overwhelmed. By that time I was unaware of anything else except the music, neither the bald man in front of me, nor the man with the book of music on his knee, nor the candelabra, nor the walls, nor the portraits on the walls.

But the thing that was really surprising was that the music I was listening to did not remind me of anything. It didn't conjure up any pictures. With an effort of course I could imagine something to myself, a picture I had seen somewhere showing a storm at sea, with broken masts and people clinging on to them. Or perhaps war would have fitted the music better. But no, I would only have been deceiving myself, inventing things, while I could already sense that this music was truthful to the core, with no cheating about it. No, storms and war wouldn't do. . . .

(What else then? In those days I couldn't work it out. But now after I've seen a bit of life, now that I've heard "Poem of Ecstasy" a hundred times and can conduct the whole thing, all twenty-two minutes of it, to myself with my eyes shut and without even raising a finger as I do it, now I know that there is something more formidable than a storm at sea, and that something is an outpouring of human feelings.)

It was as if through a dream that I heard a bell ring out, an organ sigh and all the drums explode one after the other.

Then all was calm: but I couldn't believe it. It looked as if nobody else could either, because everyone just sat there stock-still.

That was just as it should have been, because the music wasn't over, that incredible calm was still part of the music, bars of silence. Gathering up its last reserves of strength the orchestra struck up again. The conductor rallied the exhausted players with his all-powerful wand, and the stalwart musicians managed to find the energy to play on to the end and even round everything off with a joyful mighty chord.

It was only then that the whole concert-hall was filled with thunderous applause. The conductor turned to the audience and bowed. This time it was different, he'd deserved it now.

The violinists started to tap their bows on their music-stands, but as they did so they did not look at the conductor but to the back rows of the orchestra. And then the conductor himself started clapping, looking for someone in the back row of his troop.

The woman in high-heeled shoes appeared again and said: "This performance of 'Poem of Ecstasy' marks the sixtieth birthday of our gifted trumpeter, the one and only Dmitri Kuznetsov who joined the orchestra forty years ago today."

Then right at the back, the man who'd been playing the trumpet, the one to whom I'd wanted to show a lemon, rose and shuffling awkwardly started to make his way forward through the rows of music-stands urged on by the knocking bows.

He came forward and bowed clumsily. He obviously hadn't often had to take bows in front of an audience. The conductor jumped down from his dais and they hugged each other.

I looked around me again. The stickler had put his book of music away and was clapping for all he was worth. The strict-looking woman with the lace collar had tears in her eyes.

Then I heard the bald man sitting in front of me lean over to his neighbour and say: "Dmitri's retiring. That's that . . . there'll never be another Dmitri."

* * *

We went home from the concert on foot: after all it wasn't very far. Just follow your nose up

 Herzen Street, past Nikitskiye Gates, and as far as Sadovaya Ring along Herzen Street, then across the Ring and there's Krasnaya Presnya and our school.

It was neither a crocodile, nor a cluster that we made as we walked along, but a wedge-shaped group stretching across a good block, all of us trying to keep in view both the head and tail of the procession.

All the boys were talking amongst themselves as they walked along. I could hear two of them arguing: "But so what? In Shostakovich's Fifth the kettledrum's got a solo!"

"OK, but that's Shostakovich and nowadays. But for those days! Don't forget Rimsky-Korsakov heard 'Poem of Ecstasy'."

"No, he didn't."

"But he did! Scriabin played it to him on the piano. But Rimsky-Korsakov did not like it."

Those were boys from the senior forms, but I didn't understand what they were arguing about. Indeed I hardly knew them, for they didn't come to early choir practices any more.

Then we came out into Vosstaniye Square. The heavy mass of the now familiar sky-scraper loomed up over it. The topmost pinnacle kept fading from view and then reappearing as wisps of cloud floated past it. The clouds were moving fast, scurrying across the sky. The underneaths were yellow, catching the glow of the town lights. Then for a moment there was a gap in the clouds and we could see the wintry sky above them full of bright stars. Then another cloud hid them from view again.

"Ta-tu-um, ta-tu-um, ta-ta-ta-ta-ta. . . ." What was it?

It was the voice of the trumpet, the one that

had been making itself known all the time and colliding with the rest of the orchestra. That very same trumpet on which Merited Artist Dmitri had excelled himself at his farewell concert.

Yes, it was the trumpet's voice. But it wasn't a proper tune, was it? What made it spring to my mind so clearly all of a sudden? Can one really remember things that aren't tunes at all? And if you do remember them, can you reproduce them?

I covered my mouth with my woollen muffler (so that nobody should catch me singing outside in the cold, for you could be given a proper old telling-off for that) and started blowing away.

"Ta-tu-um, ta-tu-um, ta-ta-ta-ta-ta. . . ."

"Was ist das?"

"Wha-a-at?"

Two enormous figures loomed in front of me; they were the senior boys who had been talking about Shostakovich.

"Come on, do it again," commanded one of them.

"Encore!"

I made an attempt to slip away between them for I was frightened that they'd split on me to the director about my singing out in the cold. But they caught hold of my collar and again commanded a repeat performance.

There was nothing I could do. I noticed that all the others and the teachers in charge had left us far behind and that made me a little braver.

"Ta-tu-um, ta-tu-um, ta-ta-ta-ta-ta. . . . Ta-tu-um, ta-tu-um!" I sang out, fairly loudly by this time, imitating the powerful voice of the trumpet.

Then I got a flick on the nose, but not one that hurt. The boys gave each other a knowing look and then one of them inquired of the other:

"He'll do."

"Yes," pronounced the other in a solemn tone.

Then I got another flick on the nose and they walked on as if nothing had happened, while I hurried along to catch up with the rest of the first-formers.

PART TWO

1

On the way upstairs there was a mirror, or rather it was on the landing between the first and the second flight. It was a large mirror in an ebony frame and it was as wide as the landing wall. The mirror itself was tarnished and chipped and the quicksilver was wearing away at the edges, because it was very ancient, a hundred years old.

But you could still see yourself in it though. I remember how, when I first came to the school and joined the first form, I had to climb up almost as far as the top step before I was able to see myself in that mirror.

Yet now all I needed to do was to leap up half a dozen stairs and the top of my head appeared in the mirror and then my forehead, my nose, my mouth and my long neck followed and my shoulders that were rather narrow, although I was no weakling, and then I could see myself in it as far down as my waist.

I stopped for a minute by the mirror, spat on my comb and straightened up my parting; then I made sure the knot of my Young Pioneer tie was in the right place and pulled myself up a fraction. . . .

Zhenya Prokhorov, twelve years of age, in Form VI: not top of the class, but in the top ten.

What else was of interest on that particular day? It was the day of another concert in the Grand Hall of the Conservatoire. You might think that we'd just been jogging along for another five years and were back in square one, without much to show for those five years. . . .

Well, not quite! For that day the concert at the Conservatoire was not just any old concert, but *our* concert, a concert given by the Boys' Choir.

Tickets had been sold out long since as usual. There had been crowds clustering round the ticket offices since early morning and people armed with arm-twisting notes trying to worm their way into the manager's office. Then in the evening all up and down Herzen Street there would be people asking: "Any spare tickets?" and some of the passers-by would teasingly reply: "Yes, for the bath-house."

People always enjoy our concerts, and, to be honest, we enjoyed giving them. Several hours before the concert the matrons at the hostel would unlock the holy cupboard and bring out our best suits that were carefully stored away on hangers inside. Then they'd hand out clean shirts and ironed ties and shoes; those shoes we used to have to polish till you could see your face in them, but the task was a pleasant one when you knew that you would soon be scrutinised by a great hallful of people.

One of the most exciting moments was when the bus with a board marked PRIVATE on it drove in through the gates of the school. The doors would open with a whoosh all ready for us to jump in.

By the time I was twelve there had been a lot of concerts in imposing buildings with names that you always have to write in capital letters: the Hall of Columns in the House of Unions, the Red Banner Hall in the Central Club of the Soviet Army, the Central House of Culture for Railway Workers and the Tchaikovsky Concert Hall.

I suppose we ought to have got used to it all with time, but it was no good, it was impossible not to get excited every time.

As for that particular evening I had a special reason for feeling excited. A fortnight beforehand Vladimir Konstantinovich had announced: "Zhenya Prokhorov will sing the solos at the next concert, 'The Legend of Dobrynya Nikitich' and 'The Young Eagle'."

* * *

But to go back to the beginning. . . .

It was Monday, just another Monday. On Mondays we were all taken to the doctor, to the ears-nose-and-throat man or rather woman, Maria Leontyevna. In a corner of the grounds there was a tumble-down little building, the school's first-aid post. Outside the little house was terribly shabby and dirty and inside it was sparkling white and clean, complete with gleaming medical apparatus and instruments.

One by one we went up to the plate on which were laid out specially prepared pieces of lint: each one of us had to take a piece of lint and then when his turn came round sit down in the special chair, put it on the end of his tongue and pull out his tongue as far as it would go: "Ah-a-ah. . .".

When we had first come to the school and started going to Maria Leontyevna's weekly inspections, she had not looked down our throats: she had just given out pieces of lint and then sat down on a bench while we had to just sit there like little idiots with our tongues poking out, so that we shouldn't be frightened of her and get used to the ritual. By the time I had got to Form VI we were no longer frightened and quite used to it.

Maria Leontyevna used to have a round mirror attached to a band round her forehead which reflected the horribly bright light from a lamp she held up in front of our mouths into which she then pushed a laryngoscope—a long nickel-plated stem with another tiny round mirror on the end of it.

"Ah-a-ah. . . ."

"Fine, Zhenya. You can go now. Next, please."

I got down out of the chair and threw my piece of lint into the kidney-dish.

"Ah-a-ah. . ." went the next person.

"Well, well," said Maria Leontyevna and putting her laryngoscope away she leant down to take a closer look at the patient's shoes.

"Aliev, where did you get your feet wet? Have you been running through puddles?"

"No, I haven't," said Marat Aliev indignantly looking Maria Leontyevna straight in the eye with that wistful gaze of his.

(Actually he was lying. I myself had seen him running through puddles only the day before.)

"Yes, you have. This mirror shows me quite clearly that you have," said the doctor. "Vladimir Konstantinovich, Marat Aliev is not to go to choir practice for a week."

Vladimir Konstantinovich who was sitting next to me threw a stern glance at Marat from behind his spectacles.

By that time boys from the senior classes were waiting at the door to come in. Kolya Biryukov's turn came round and he took his place in the chair. Kolya Biryukov, who was no longer Nikolai Ivanovich to me by then, had grown still more enormous in the meantime and his mouth was broader than ever.

"Ah-a-ah. . . ."

From a distance I admired that throat. There

was a really fine throat for you! It was a real fright of a mouth, it was so enormous!

"Wider."

"Ah-a-ah...."

Maria Leontyevna looked long and hard into that throat and then she turned to Vladimir Konstantinovich again asking him to come and have a look too.

She shifted the lamp and Vladimir Konstantinovich bent over to peer down Kolya's throat.

"Ah-a-ah...."

"Can you see?"

"Yes ... yes...."

Maria Leontyevna put her laryngoscope down and stated adamantly: "He mustn't do any singing."

Kolya Biryukov snapped his mouth shut, and his lips closed tight in a sullen scowl. Then Vladimir Konstantinovich took off his spectacles and started to give them a thorough wipe with his handkerchief. Then he added in a quiet voice:

"Maria Leontyevna, on the twenty-sixth there's going to be a concert."

"Biryukov mustn't sing and solos are quite out of the question."

"Perhaps I'll be all right by the twenty-sixth?" asked Kolya hopefully.

"No, you won't. It's going to be a long business, Kolya."

The director turned away looking over to the window.

Biryukov jumped out of the chair and ran out of the room.

"Next, please."

"Ah-a-ah...."

"Fine, Igor. Very good. . . . Next, please."
"Ah-a-ah."
"Fine."

* * *

And how he sang!

We could all sing, otherwise we wouldn't have been kept on at the school, in fact we all sang well and each of us was being trained as a potential soloist.

But, to be honest, Kolya Biryukov sang better than anybody else. His voice was quite remarkable and ever since I had been at the school it had been he who had done the solos. There had even been the time when Kolya Biryukov had sung a solo not at our choir's concert, but at a concert with a real grown-up choir. I had seen the posters stuck up all round Moscow that said: "Soloist—N. Biryukov."

So it's not difficult to imagine what Maria Leontyevna's harsh sentence—"He mustn't sing" —meant for Kolya. Nor is it difficult to imagine how unexpected it was for me to be told at choir practice: "Zhenya Prokhorov will sing the solos at the concert, 'The Legend of Dobrynya Nikitich' and 'The Young Eagle'."

I had known the solo parts for those two songs for some time, yet I still had to practice them till I was blue in the face, both with the choir and on my own, with Sergei Pavlovich. He too had once been a choir-boy at our school, not here in Moscow though but in Leningrad, where the school had originally been founded. When the war began and the Germans laid siege to Leningrad the boys had been evacuated to the village of Arbazh near Kirov, where they lived and carried on with their lessons and their singing. Sergei Pavlovich also told us how bad the food situation was there. Even after the Germans had been driven away from Leningrad it wasn't possible to take the boys back to the city—things were still in a terrible state even after the siege had been lifted. It was then that the school had moved to Moscow, to Bolshaya Gruzinskaya Street. Nowadays there are two choir schools, Leningrad and Moscow both have one of their own. It's really astonishing how the years pass and wars come and go and boys just go on and on singing. When one lot set off for the wars their successors went on singing.

I also learnt that Vladimir Konstantinovich had once been in a boys' choir too, but a church choir. I found it difficult to imagine though how he, our director, had looked at singing practice as a small boy, being shouted at by a bearded precentor: "You there, what's your name . . . Namestnikov, isn't it? Rounder on those top notes . . . more tone!"

That must have been a laugh.

Then our old Namestnikov had taught Sergei Pavlovich, the accompanist, who himself is starting to go grey too. For some reason he didn't become a famous singer, nor a celebrated pianist. It must have been because out there in Arbazh village during the war the boys had had such scant rations. Or perhaps he just wanted to be an accompanist and work in the school where he himself had learnt to sing.

I liked practicing with Sergei Pavlovich because he knows so much and has such a sensitive ear. It always seems as if every note that I sing, he sings too but inside himself, deep down in those grey eyes of his.

"You're ready for the big moment now," said Sergei Pavlovich on the eve of the concert.

"Yes, I should think so," agreed Vladimir Konstantinovich after he had listened too.

But when we all took our seats in the bus to leave for the concert hall I caught sight of Kolya Biryukov on the back seat, his shoulders hunched and the peak of his beaver-lamb cap pulled down low over his forehead. He wasn't looking at me: he wasn't looking at anybody. He was looking out of the window.

To this day I don't know why he went with us that evening, although he had been strictly forbidden to sing. Perhaps he had asked permission or perhaps not bothered. Perhaps he was coming along in case of an emergency, in case I should suddenly lose my nerve, or perhaps it was out of curiosity, to see whether I would make a go of it at the first attempt.

The only other thing I ought to mention was that Biryukov's presence in the bus did not escape Vladimir Konstantinovich although Kolya had pulled his cap well down over his eyes. The director noticed him at once but didn't say anything.

After all getting unused to something takes just as long as getting used to it.

* * *

That evening we were singing our usual repertoire: Haydn's "Advent of Spring", a Bach trio, Lyadov's "Cradle Song", Palestrina's "In the Heavens" and various works by modern composers. The modern numbers in our repertoire were periodically changed, after all it was an important part of our work to popularise new music, but Bach, Lyadov and Palestrina appeared every time without fail and will probably always do so.

Just look at Giovanni Palestrina for instance: he lived four hundred years ago, *four hundred*!... And his song "In the Heavens" was specially written for a boys' choir at that time.

Greetings, Giovanni Palestrina! We're still singing your song to this day.

We sing your song.

People listen to us with bated breath.

They sit transfixed, afraid to move a muscle.

It was a great pity, it really was, that I couldn't see our choir from out there in the audience. It probably made a fine sight, with the straight rows of boys all dressed identically. The rows were arranged in order of height, the smallest boys in the front and the tallest ones at the very back. (I was about in the middle.) And I can imagine how behind the lankiest of all towered up the silver pipes of the organ, the famous Conservatoire organ, like a perfectly natural continuation of the back row of boys. Probably the people sitting out in front saw all the rows of the boys and the organ as one whole, it must have seemed to them that the organ was pealing forth in its brilliant upper registers.

Like all the others I was concentrating hard on the particular part I was meant to be singing, but nevertheless I was able to pick out various individual voices: Marat Aliev who had sat out his week of banishment from singing practice, Georgi Vyazemsky and there went Vitya Titarenko—all my classmates.

But however hard I listened I couldn't pick out a familiar voice, and the one I liked best of all, Kolya Biryukov's. It was not to be heard although

I had seen him take his place with the others in the back row.

So they hadn't let him sing after all, which meant that I really would have to sing the solo.

Oh dear audience, most kind concert-goers! . . . Do you really insist? What on earth d'you want to hear my solo for? Isn't the choir's harmonious singing good enough for you? What a beautiful thing choral singing is. The finest work of all for a good singer is to sing in a well-balanced choir, rubbing shoulders with his friends, Vitya Titarenko, Georgi Vyazemsky and Marat Aliev.

What do you need a stupid old solo for? Surely you can do without it!

" 'The Legend of Dobrynya Nikitich'," came the voice of the announcer. "The solo will be sung by Zhenya Prokhorov."

I bowed my head and stepped forward from my place in the neat row. Farewell, friends. . . .

There I was out in front of the choir. A little further out in front and slightly to one side was Vladimir Konstantinovich. He was in tails and wearing a stiff white shirt-front and a white bow-tie.

He bent right over towards me. And there had I been boasting about how much I'd grown during the last few years, how I'd fairly shot up. Yet here was he, conductor Namestnikov, having to bend down towards me as if I was nothing but a tiny gnome. It wasn't really because of me though, it was just that he was incredibly tall and skinny like a pole.

He then stretched out his hands with their bony fingers in front of him, till they almost touched my face. . . .

I was terribly scared by then and my knees started to shake. Those long sallow fingers in front of me frightened me much more than the hushed quiet out there in the audience. Not really frightened I suppose, it was just that I had got used to obeying them without a murmur, like a command from on high. Then my knees stopped shaking which was most fortunate for if they had gone on shaking they would have made my voice shake too and the end result would have been nothing better than some hideous little-bleats.

The old hands slowly rose. . . .

It is no birch tree that bows to the earth
Nor silken grass that bends low. . .

Saved again, the first phrases had gone without mishap, as they had at rehearsal. At rehearsals though I had only been singing in the small hall at school. I had never heard my own voice all by itself in such a wealth of space as this hall of the Conservatoire which not for nothing is known as the Grand Hall. How horrifyingly far away were the back rows, how distant and high up the balcony seemed. Yet there were people right up there, who'd paid money to come. Could they hear me, I wondered?

Yet even by that stage I felt sure they could. I didn't even try to strain my voice, something that we were strictly forbidden to do anyway. Nevertheless I felt quite sure that I could be heard in the very back rows because I had a voice that carried astonishingly far. Even if I were to sing something very softly, pianissimo, it would have been heard all the same. Yes, it would have been heard, without any microphones or loudspeakers too.

Before his mother, homage to show
Bows a son. . .

The conductor's hand came to rest on his chest, on his white shirt-front. I grasped what that meant: first of all: "Zhenya, sing from your diaphragm, like that, that's fine", second: "Zhenya, put more feeling into it... remember it's a son bidding farewell to his mother", and third: "Zhenya, keep your O's round, proper O's not A sounds."

I grasped all that at once and tried to follow the directions. I tried to sing from my diaphragm and thought people couldn't fail to notice how deep down those notes were. I pictured to myself a son bidding farewell to his mother. I also had a mother once and I try and bid farewell to her. When it came to the word "bows" I made my O sound as round as I possibly could.

Then the whole choir came in. At the end loud applause broke out. Then I took my bow—this time not in the words of a song, but the real thing. I bowed to the audience as I had been taught to do at the last few rehearsals.

The next song, Bely's "The Young Eagle", was announced, at which Sergei Pavlovich appeared at the piano, for that song was to be accompanied. It was a modern song by a Soviet composer. I don't really know whether it appeals to the taste of strict connoisseurs of the classic repertoire, but it's a real favourite with our boys.

I started off:

Little eagle, to the sun take wing,
Look down on the steppe below:
No more will the merry peasants sing;
I am left alone with my woe...

Then all of a sudden I felt things go tight in my chest. It was almost as if a lump had come into my throat. But that was out of the question:

 there could be no lumps! I was in the middle of singing and my throat had to be clear and free. But I couldn't help how I felt!

I love that song, its stern, honest words. Then the tune is wonderful. I'd noticed soon after I'd first heard it the impressive build-up to the high notes: it soars and falls again as if on wings, ever higher. . . .

I love "The Young Eagle" and often used to ponder over it, and wonder how the composer had come to write it? Was it just a lucky piece of inspiration, a sudden outpouring of his soul? Or had the arrangement of those melodic passages, the sequence of high notes and transitions from one key to another been a long, tortuous process?

Before I knew where I was we had come to the end of "The Young Eagle".

I had the impression that I had sung my solo all right, no worse than Kolya Biryukov.

What the audience got up to after that though was nobody's business! . . . and in the stately and imposing Grand Hall of the Conservatoire at that!

I took my bow and went back to my place in the middle row of the choir, but the audience went on clapping most frenziedly. Vladimir Konstantinovich made a sign to me to go out and bow again (although he himself was very much against ovations, encores and the like. That was because he Namestnikov was first and foremost a teacher and knew all too well how misguided it was on the audience's part to give such ovations and encore performers like me who were hardly out of nappies).

Yet he still made the sign to me to go out and take another bow and I meekly obeyed.

At that moment a girl in one of the back rows

got up and ran right up the main gangway to the stage. She was wearing a pink dress and had pink ribbons in her hair and she was carrying a bouquet of flowers, daffodils I think. Standing up on tiptoe she put the bouquet down at my feet, by my glistening shoes, and ran back to her place.

I stood there wishing I could sink through the floor.

The audience went on clapping though, enough to make their hands quite sore.

Vladimir Konstantinovich obviously forcing himself to adopt a benign smile—that was for the audience's sake of course—made another sign to me: this time to say as much as pick up your flowers seeing you've been given them, be sharp about it and get back to your place; tomorrow I shall have a few words with you, Zhenya Prokhorov, in my study.

I bent down, picked up the unfortunate bouquet and suddenly a note folded into a small square fell out of the flowers onto the floor. I blushed as red as a lobster and by this time the audience was laughing as if they were at the circus rather than the Conservatoire.

Vladimir Konstantinovich looked straight down at me with such a calm expression that it left no room for doubt any more: if all that hadn't happened nowadays after the Revolution, but before, he would have had me flogged that evening.

I picked the note up off the floor, stuck it hastily into my breast pocket, went back to my place and hid from view behind other people's backs.

" 'The Echo' by Orlando Lasso," came the announcer's voice.

* * *

After the concert came eats.

The thing was that we weren't paid for those concerts we gave, despite all the people that flocked to them. Perhaps the choir school got some percentage or other (I wasn't very well up in the financial side of it all), but we choir-boys who put on the show were not of course paid. Indeed it would have been strange if we had had to sign wage slips at that tender age.

But celebration eats were laid on after every concert—they were part of the whole sacred ritual. A long table covered with a white tablecloth was covered with dishes of oranges and cakes, plates of cheese and sausage sandwiches, little bowls of sweets and glasses of steaming hot tea. It was a sight to make your mouth water.

We hurled ourselves at the goodies as if we had had nothing to eat for an age, although to be honest none of us was underfed. We had perfectly good meals with decent-sized helping three times a day at school and those who wanted more were never refused seconds.

Besides our school did not only take in boys like me who came from orphanages and who had no parents. Some of them had parents, had mummies and daddies blooming with health, who lived in other towns though and who used to send their sons food parcels: for instance Marat Aliev used to receive such sumptuous parcels from his parents in the Caucasus that there was enough for the whole hostel to tuck into, still leaving plenty for Marat. Better still, though, there were some children whose parents actually lived in Moscow itself and those children when they had finished their lessons for the day were able to go home and spend the night there before appearing for the next day's lessons. Those day-boys you could easily pick out from the rest, although we all used to wear one and the same uniform. Even so their shoes were a shade more fashionable than our standard ones and their shirts whiter, their school-bags plusher and their pens flashier. That all made us assume that at home they were not exactly fed on bread and water. We imagined that they were able to wallow in sausage and cheese. Despite the fact that none of us had any real cause for complaint in the food line, as soon as the eats appeared after each concert we all hurled ourselves at the plates and dishes of food with as much frantic eagerness as if we had just been rescued from a desert island.

The waitresses and refreshment sellers stood to one side watching us with expressions of compassion on their faces, shaking their heads as we gorged ourselves.

To be fair I must confess that I threw myself just as wildly at the sandwiches and tea as everybody else. On that occasion I found myself sitting opposite Nikolai Ivanovich Biryukov who was putting his enormous jaws to good use although that evening he had not sung a single note. Perhaps he had only come for the sake of the food, who knows? . . .

Kolya Biryukov looked at me and all of a sudden his jaws stopped working. In astonishment I too stopped munching. Kolya raised his eye-brows in a strange fashion, craned his neck forward and started looking me straight in the eye. I put my hand up to my cheek: perhaps I had got a smear on my face somewhere? But he went on staring at me, obviously excited about something.

"Zhenya, what is it you've got there?"

"Where?" I asked, really alarmed by that time.

"You know. . . ."

At that Nikolai Ivanovich rose a little from his chair, bent across the table and with a still more excited look than before scrutinised my face.

"But what is it?" I inquired, starting to finger my nose and my forehead.

At that moment Kolya Biryukov's hand dipped cheekily into my breast pocket and grabbed hold of the note inside. That wretched note. . . . It wasn't that I had forgotten about it, simply that I hadn't had the chance to have a look and see what was written in it on my own without other people around.

I jumped up and lunged out to snatch it back but then someone came up behind me and took firm hold of me by the shoulders. I could sense that it was Vitya Titarenko and I knew there was no hope of escaping his clutches: his grip was an iron one and he was the strongest boy in the class. I couldn't move an inch.

By that time Kolya Biryukov had unfolded the blasted little note and was declaiming its contents for the whole table to relish: "My name is Maya. My telephone number is. . . ."

"Stop!" came a voice at the other end of the table. It was Georgi Vyazemsky, a curly-haired, rosy-cheeked boy also from our class.

"Stop!" he ordered in a tone of command.

"What d'you want then?" asked Nikolai Ivanovich with a frown.

"Now I'm going to show you some telepathy," announced Georgi. "You will now witness some thought-reading and I shall read that note from here without looking at it. I can guess the telephone number that's in the note. Who'll take me on? With their cream-cake for a stake?"

"Go on, get on with it," said Kolya and hid the note in his clenched fist. "I'll bet you my cream-cake, but you'll have to pay up in money, OK?"

"All right," replied Georgi with a nod.

"I'll take you on as well," came another voice over to the left. "I'll bet you an éclair. You couldn't possibly guess it!"

"Me too!" someone else chipped in excitedly from over on the right.

All this time I was struggling to break free from Vitya's hold.

Then Georgi pushed his curls back from off his forehead, put one hand over his eyes and stretched out the other in front of him with his fingers wide apart and making groping movements in the air said: "D-three. . . ." Kolya opened his fist and took a look at the piece of paper.

"Double-O. . . ."

By now a few more heads had bent over the note.

"Eighty-two!"

A stunned silence came over the whole table. So he must have guessed the right number after all.

"Please would you pass along the three cream-cakes," commanded Georgi.

Kolya, twiddling the note in his fingers, sighed and put his untouched éclair on a plate with the two others, and the plate made its way up to the far end of the table. At last Vitya let go of my shoulders.

To make sure of his prize Georgi bit off the end of all three éclairs.

"By the way, it was my sister," he announced, and then gulping down his tea he added: "Little fool."

2

The concert had been on a Saturday and on Sunday morning, a week after that, Kolya Biryukov came up to me. He hadn't been near me once for the whole of the week, he had been actually ignoring me as if I had ceased to exist.

He came up to me and said: "Let's get out of here for a bit, Prokhorov."

"Where to?"

"Let's go and look at some animals. Birds. Fishes. Tortoises."

"To the Zoo?" I asked not very keen.

I was fed to the teeth with the Zoo by then. I had probably been a hundred times to that jolly Zoo right outside our windows since Nikolai Ivanovich Biryukov had taken me there my first day in Moscow. And now again! . . .

"No, not to the Zoo," replied Kolya, shaking his head. "To the Bird Market. Coming?"

"Where's that?"

"I'll show you where."

"But what for?"

"Just to have a look round."

"OK," I said.

And why not, after all? It was Sunday and the Bird Market was somewhere I had never been before, although I'd been to lots of museums and the planetarium.

"Let's go then," I said.

We set off and took the Metro to Taganskaya Station; after that we took a trolleybus and then a few minutes more on foot brought us to the Bird Market.

It turned out that the Bird Market wasn't its proper name at all: it was really Kalitnikovsky

Market, or at least that was what was written up over the gate. I also learnt that the market only functioned at weekends and on public holidays and the rest of the time it was locked up.

But at weekends . . . wow, it was full!

There was such a frantic crowd and such hustling and bustling that we had quite a job to get inside and the further we went the worse it got. I soon noticed that the Bird Market had precious little to do with birds. Fish Market would have been more appropriate, for everywhere you turned, everywhere you looked, there were nothing but fish to be seen. There were rows and rows of glass jars on all the stalls and in them were swimming and cavorting cute little fish—red ones, black ones, striped ones—the lot.

Business was lively not only at the actual stalls but in the crowd as well. Nearly everybody, grown-ups and children alike, was armed with a jar. With the help of little nets fish were being lifted out of one jar into another and money was changing hands at lightning speed.

Apart from actual fish all kinds of paraphernalia you need for keeping fish was also changing hands: aquariums decorated with all kinds of shells, live worms and slugs all a-wriggle, and dry forms of fish food. You could even buy seaweed and snails. There were special electric air-pumps. One man was selling sand, pouring it into little bags at fifty kopecks a time, if you please! There was another (and I saw him with my own eyes) selling water: he filled his bucket from an ordinary tap in the yard and then walked round the market calling: "Who needs genuine lake water? Water straight from a lake!" And what's more there were people who actually bought some, I saw them doing it.

In a word Kolya and I found ourselves in a kind of fish kingdom.

Only in a remote corner right over by the back fence were there people selling other things apart from fish. There were some cages with canaries and goldfinches, pigeons in plywood boxes, and then we came across hampers with rabbits and guinea-pigs. It was all most fascinating and Kolya and I probably spent a good two hours pottering round.

"And no-o-ow..." said Kolya and led me over to the exit.

"What now?"

"Now we come to the best part of all."

"What d'you mean?" I asked in surprise. Here he was going on about the best thing of all and leading me away from the whole show over to the gate. After we got outside we walked along by the fence, and soon enough I realised where he was taking me... to the dog section.

The little alley-way we went into resounded with barking in all different keys, growls, yaps and whimpers that didn't let up for a second. There was every kind of dog you cared to think of!—fully-grown dogs and puppies with their eyes only just open and still wobbly on their pins, square-nosed thoroughbred boxers and hairy mongrels. There were setters and tiny little chihuahuas. Finding themselves all of a sudden in that enormous colourful crowd they were behaving noisily and mischievously. They kept on jumping all over each other, starting up fights or else sniffing and nuzzling each other or seeing which of them could lift their leg highest at the fence.

Buyers and sellers were behaving just as noisily and excitedly. They were haggling as was to be expected at a market. There was a continual coming and going as people went to check on pedigree certificates, made a thorough inspection of the dogs' bites, shaking their heads knowingly as they discussed the animals' pros and cons.

A couple of times a woman walked past us in a blue coat with the top button undone: through the gap were peeping little white faces with rosy pink noses that belonged to a sweet and quaint little pair of twin puppies. They of course don't really count as proper dogs—they're nothing but ornaments or mere toys.

"Look!" exclaimed Nikolai giving me a nudge.

I looked in the direction he was pointing and there at the far end of the alley-way was sitting an enormous black dog with a tan belly: it was an Alsatian with a broad chest and pointed ears. There was a whole string of medals hanging from his collar, ten or more and all of them gold. Unlike all his fellows on that bustling Sunday morning he was not barking or getting up to mischief but sat there serene and dignified, his face turned away from his master. The owner was a young man of about twenty with a shaved head and he too was looking away from the dog. The expressions in the eyes of the dog and his master were equally sad.

That fine prize-winning dog had already sensed that his master wanted to sell him and was in the process of doing so. Of course he didn't want to be sold, he couldn't even imagine that anyone could sell him and hand him over to an unfamiliar stranger. But probably he had understood at the same time that if his master had decided to sell him then there must have been some special and very important reasons for it and that he the dog must be obedient to his master even here at the market and do as he was told without question.

Meanwhile the dog's master, the lad with the shaven head, himself was almost crying at the thought that he would have to sell his wonderful loyal dog. Perhaps he had nowhere to keep him, perhaps he had just been called up for his military service or had to set off to a place where he couldn't take the dog, or his neighbours had complained to the militia that he barked and drowned their television sets. Or perhaps he just had no money and was in terrible need of some, to see his mother through an illness or something like that, so that he had decided to make the supreme sacrifice although he realised how unkind it was of him, not to say treacherous.

The young man was holding a lead the other end of which was attached to the dog's collar but the lead hung slackly and although it still linked the two of them in a way, it was only really for appearance's sake. The dog and the man were looking sadly in opposite directions, as if they were trying to avoid each other.

I just couldn't take my eyes off the splendid beast.

"Fantastic, isn't he?" said Kolya.

"Yes," I agreed. "I wonder what his name is."

After pausing for a second Kolya strolled towards the boy with the shaved head and asked him something. It must have been about the dog's name or else how much he cost. But the owner of the dog merely looked at him sideways over his shoulder, spat and said some short phrase. Clearly nothing flattering though. I couldn't make it out from where I was standing.

An offended Kolya came back to join me and

seizing me by the hand he pulled me away from all the dogs.

"Fool," he said with regard to the Alsatian's owner. "Idiot. He thinks I can't buy the dog, but I *can*."

"Oh, sure thing!" I scoffed at him, doubting his wealth in my turn.

"I can. Don't you believe me then?"

Kolya stopped and after taking a cautious look around him he opened some inside pocket of his and took out a wad of notes. My eyes nearly popped out of my head at the sight of it.

"Where d'you get that lot from?" I asked.

"It's from my grant money," said Kolya with a proud laugh. "I've been saving up for a whole year."

The boys in the senior classes really did receive a grant of sorts (apart from those with very low marks and those who skipped lessons) but it was far from large. I was astonished to think that Kolya Biryukov had been able to save such an imposing sum from it.

"So you see, if I take it into my head to buy a dog, I *shall* be able to buy one," said Kolya. "That dog we saw, or any dog."

"But where would you keep it? They'd never let you into the hostel with it."

"Who said anything about the hostel! I could find work as a watchman at someone's country-house for the winter, me and the dog. Or I could just get on a train and chug away to the ends of the earth. I can do anything now. I've got the money."

"But you've got another two years to do at school," I said trying to make him see reason.

"At school?" Kolya looked at me with undisguised pity as he said that. Then he spat on the ground like the owner of the dog had.

"What for?" he went on.

"What d'you mean 'what for'?"

"Well, what for?"

There's a tickler. How does one answer that one? Why stay on at school, he's asking. . . . Everyone knows why . . . everyone stays on at school.

We were walking through a square at that moment where there were some benches, although rather damp ones. Kolya suggested: "Let's sit down."

We sat down and he began: "Listen, Zhenya . . . don't you start getting the wrong end of the stick. You probably think I'm doing this out of spite. But it's quite the opposite. It's just that I don't like the way little fellows are being had."

"Who's having us on?"

"They."

"What do you mean?"

"You see, Zhenya, it takes quite a bit of explaining." Nikolai Ivanovich frowned as if what he had to say was going to be unpleasant and difficult for him. "It's a serious matter."

I lowered my head and made ready to listen to what would follow. Well, if it's a serious matter he had better get on with it. It wasn't the first time I'd had to listen to all kinds of conversations which senior boys liked starting up with us juniors. And they'd be making fun of us at the same time too saying we were little twits who didn't know anything. . . . And they'd tell you such things as would make you ashamed to look people in the eye again. Yet nobody else tells us younger boys about such things or offers any other version to take the place of those stories. So all we can do is try and find things out for ourselves, glean snippets of knowledge from the other boys.

I was sure that Kolya was about to tell me something horrible and that was why I bowed my head and leant my face on my hands so that it wouldn't show if I blushed.

"D'you know why I wasn't allowed to sing? It's because of puberty, and what is puberty? D'you know? You don't... well puberty is when we become men. You haven't got to that stage yet, but I am changing."

All right....

"Well, when puberty comes you mustn't sing, because your voice starts to break. It takes a very long time for someone's voice to break, a whole year. It's like a disease but not one that you catch from germs, it's just, well, a law of nature. If you're a treble now, later after you've reached puberty you'll have a bass. If you're an alto, then you'll become a tenor. D'you get?"

"Well? So what?" I asked with more lively interest, taking my hands off my cheeks. I could relax now, for I realised that Kolya wasn't going to tell me anything horrible. "So what?" I went on. "You've got a treble voice and I've got a treble voice so that means we'll have bass voices later on. That's splendid...."

I stood up, stuck my stomach out, raised my eyebrows in a comical fashion and started up in a throaty voice:

Dread death my sword spread wide...

But Kolya Biryukov looked at me with undisguised pity.

"No, it doesn't," he said in a harsh voice.

"What d'you mean?"

"I mean we won't have any kind of voice."

"What! None at all?"

"Well, we'll still be able to talk of course, bla-bla-bla."

"And for singing?"

"We won't have a singing voice any more."

"Why?"

"We just won't, it's a law of nature," repeated Nikolai Ivanovich. "I for instance won't have a voice worth listening to any more. I can sense it, you see. And you won't have one either, Zhenya. . . . But don't you get sore at me: I'm playing it straight with you, from one friend to another, so that you should know before it happens."

"Well, suppose you are right," I said, thinking it over. "But where do singers spring from then? Real singers, the kind that sing at the opera-house or on the radio. Where do they spring from?"

"You're a strange fish, you really are! They don't sing like that from the word go. Their voices are discovered later, after they're grown up, and then they're there for life. But just think for a minute how many of them there are, real voices! You'll find one in a thousand and not always that many. In our school there are only two hundred boys in all. How d'you think everyone of us could hope to keep his voice? It doesn't work like that, Zhenya, it's a law of nature. In our senior classes, there's no one with a voice any more. I kept going longer than all the rest because my voice broke late, but I'm croaking away like the others now."

"So no one will have a proper voice afterwards?" I said shaking my head and finding it all so hard to take in.

"Hardly anybody anyway," Kolya replied. "I only know of one boy who kept his voice and went on to become a singer, and he wasn't from our school but the Leningrad one.... It's one in a thousand."

One in a thousand.

Now I could really understand my friend Kolya Biryukov. I felt sorry for him, for it must have been a hard blow; he'd been singing away for all that time, doing the solos at concerts, his name had been up on posters in enormous letters all over the town, and then all of a sudden—bang! It was enough to make anyone feel hard done by.

And then, I thought to myself, Kolya was probably taking it a bit hard that I was now to sing the solos instead of him, that I would be in the limelight now instead of him and be offered the bouquets.

If I had been in his place I would probably have felt jealous as well. And as for the fact that not all boys keep their good singing voices after puberty that was quite true, I had been pretending when I said I didn't know, for I had heard about that a long time ago. One of the boys had told me what puberty was when I had been in my second year.

One in a thousand? Well, Kolya had been laying it on thick to impress me, to put the fear of God into me. Well, what if it is one in a thousand.... I was quite sure who that one was going to be....

"Look over there," said Kolya all of a sudden.

The boy with the shaved head was walking down the little street at a leisurely pace. At his side sauntered the enormous black and tan dog with his ears pricked, and his medals clinking as they went. They were walking away from the market.

So the boy hadn't been able to sell his dog: he

must have been asking too high a price. Well and how would he get along now without that money that he needed so badly? Or if he had to travel to the kind of place where you couldn't take dogs with you? Or if the neighbours handed in a complaint to the militia? Things would be tricky....

Yet it looked to me as if the boy going down the street wasn't too depressed after all. His face had a worried look about it still, but the expression of desperate grief had disappeared from his eyes and he didn't look as gloomy as he had standing by the fence—he looked relieved and kind now.

Meanwhile the great dog that had been walking along sedately and obediently at his master's heels suddenly for no apparent reason yapped loudly, jumped up on to his hind legs, put his front paws on the boy's shoulders and licked his cheek with his long pink tongue.

"What an animal," said Kolya admiringly.

3

One day without any warning I was called to the director's study in the middle of a history lesson.

With no idea what it was all about I went up to the high door, knocked and went in. But then I stopped dead in my tracks.

For when I went into the familiar room, there was the director at his desk and sitting there next to him as if it was quite the most natural thing in the world was Beethoven. It was enough to make anyone's head reel.

Beethoven, without noticing my entrance, went on telling the director in an excited voice:

"...he shouldn't have been allowed to take the penalty, he was too worked up. He's much too young anyway. Believe me, old hands should take penalties. If he had got that one in, it would have been his nineteenth and it would have made him the season's top scorer. It was very decent of the team to let him have that kick. It should have been a dead cert! The vital moment with the score at nil all!... But, naturally enough, he got all worked up and kicked it right into Yashin's waiting arms...."

Vladimir Konstantinovich was being the attentive listener but obviously only half his mind was on the story. In the first place I knew that our director wasn't very keen on football and he might well not have known who Yashin was, and secondly he, unlike Beethoven, had noticed me standing at the door.

"Come in," he said and introduced me to the visitor. "This is Zhenya Prokhorov. Zhenya, I hope...."

Of course he could rely on me, a pupil of his music school, not letting him down and appearing a complete nitwit. He could rest assured that I knew my composers, all the giants at least, from their pictures.

And there in the armchair was sitting a real life giant. I had immediately recognised the lean, pale face, the thin lips and the hair curling down over the top of his forehead.

Then the composer held out his hand to me and said: "Hallo. I'm glad to meet you. I heard you singing at the concert. I liked your 'Legend' —not bad."

I lowered my gaze bashfully. Who was I to argue with a giant! Not bad, but of course.

"Zhenya," he said, undoing the zip on his document case, "I've written a new song, called 'Homing Signal'. D'you know what a 'homing signal' is?"

"Yes . . ." I answered, struggling to collect my wits. "It's. . . ."

"Yes, exactly," he went on. "It's a radio signal. A constant, steady signal. When a plane is flying high at night it has to hear a constant signal from the earth, so as to keep on its course. D'you understand?"

"Yes."

"But here, apart from the technical side, the symbolism is important. It would be fine if a Soviet song could be a sort of 'homing signal'. It must be sung by a boy and I want you to sing it."

He handed me a manuscript copy of the music.

"Shall we have a run-through?"

He looked about him, but there was no piano in the director's study, only an antique harmonium.

"We can go downstairs to the music-room," suggested Vladimir Konstantinovich.

"No, no need to bother." The composer went quickly up to the harmonium and lifted the lid: "A Hofberg, very nice too . . . indeed most original."

He bent down low over the keyboard surveying the stops. Then he sat down and with obvious pleasure put his feet on the stiff pedals of the bellows. He turned to me and said: "Off we go. Can you sight-read?"

"Yes," I nodded looking at the notes and the words divided up into syllables under them.

"Let's have a run-through," he said again.

The bellows of the old harmonium started to puff away. . . .

* * *

The spool turned slowly as if reluctant to surrender coils of the brown tape to the other one next to it.

The loudspeakers let out loud pure sound:

Let the antennae,
antennae,
antennae...

That was how I first heard my own voice. I hardly recognised it. Probably even the most sensitive of microphones and the most meticulous of recordings distort the natural timbre of any voice a fraction. However, I liked the voice I heard a lot and the song too. I liked the harmonious, flowing orchestral accompaniment, indeed it was the first time I had ever sung with that kind of accompaniment. It was also the first time in my life that I had ever found myself in those particular surroundings.

This was how it all came about—two days after the composer had visited the school I had been summoned to appear at the Recording Centre. Again I was let off lessons (what a life I was leading!) and given detailed instructions as to how to get there.

It was quite easy. All I had to go was come out of the school grounds, go round the corner, cross the Sadovaya Ring, bear left, then right and there I was in Kachalov Street, where the Recording Centre was. It was no distance at all. In general our choir-school is very conveniently situated. It's handy for almost everything, a hop, skip and a jump and there you are.

I arrived at the appointed time. In the entrance hall someone looked out my name in the long list of people expected that day and wrote me out a pass.

There was an imposing and stern-looking militia-man at the door. He took my pass out of my hand, read it through, turned it over, eyed me up and down suspiciously but didn't go so far as to object, for after all it was perfectly in order, complete with a stamp, and let me through. He even saluted. Now that was really something!

I found myself in an enormous room that was so full of people it looked as if it would burst at the seams.

There were various staff running around reading pieces of paper as they went. There were violinists and flutists marching along with smart instrument cases, and a double-bass player bent double as he carried his whale of an instrument along on his back. There was a group of women in identical long white dresses that came down to the floor: they were probably from some choir or other. I was surprised to see that they were dressed like that here, seeing that when they sing on the radio they were only being heard not seen: on the other hand, though, uniform does give one a sense of discipline, that much I knew already from my own experience.

I had been told to come to Studio 1 at twelve o'clock and I was there with five minutes to spare. The studio was enormous as well. There was a whole symphony orchestra in there, happily and chaotically tuning their instruments to the loud A of the bassoon.

The conductor was already on the stand. He greeted me very kindly, patted me on the head and asked what my name was. I felt too shy, though, to ask him the same question. In the wall straight opposite the orchestra there was a wide double window, through which a bald head saddled with head-phones was to be seen.

"Let's begin then. We'll have a run-through," thundered a voice from the loudspeaker that was fixed to the wall above the wide window and I realised that it was the bald man who had given the orders from out of that glass-walled cabin, the recording engineer.

I won't go into all the details of what followed. To cut a long story short I sang the song all right, without any hitches.

Now it was being played back and the spool was spinning slowly away:

Starwards Antey,
Antey,
Antey...

We were all listening to the play-back, the conductor, the bald recording engineer and me.

When it had come to an end the conductor turned to the recording engineer and asked:

"Well, what d'you think?"

"Everything's fine," he replied.

"Yes, I'd say it didn't go at all badly," agreed the conductor. "What about you, Zhenya? Did *you* like it?"

I seized up with embarrassment and didn't know what I should answer. The thing was that it was me doing the singing, me and nobody else, and I couldn't very well praise myself. It was all the more awkward because I thought it was really hot stuff. I tried to put on an indifferent expression but instead of that my lips ran away with me and out slipped a happy smile as I said: "Yes."

Fortunately at that moment the door of the recording booth opened to let two people in, a man and a woman.

"Good afternoon," said the man and before I'd had time to take a proper look at him I jumped on recognising his voice.

It was Lemeshev's voice and there *was* Lemeshev, the famous tenor! I recognised him immediately, at first by his voice, that remarkable, inimitable voice that you couldn't help but recognise the moment you heard it even if all it was doing was saying "Good afternoon". Then I recognised his face. Although I had never had the good fortune to see Lemeshev at a concert or at the opera house I had seen the film "A Musical Story" a hundred times, in which Lemeshev played the part of a taxi-driver by the name of Petya Govorkov. He acts and sings in it. I adored that film although it was very old, pre-war even, and had been made before I was born. Naturally Lemeshev looked older now than in the days when he had played the part of Petya Govorkov the taxi-driver, who became an opera singer, but he was just as handsome all the same.

The conductor rushed over to greet him and the recording engineer rose respectfully from his chair. Lemeshev nodded at me in greeting and the woman with him patted me on the head. For some reason or other everyone was patting me on the head that day. It was a pity but I didn't know who the woman was except that she was a singer of course, and as I was soon to hear for myself, a wonderful singer. But to this day I don't know what her name was. Lemeshev just called her Tanya.

"Let's begin. All right, Tanya?"

"Yes."

The three of them went into the studio: Lemeshev, Tanya and the conductor, while I and the recording engineer stayed behind in the recording booth. Of course I realised that it was time for me to leave, that there was nothing more for me to do, that my song was sung and that was it. But I wanted terribly badly to stay behind.

"May I stay here for a bit?" I asked the recording engineer.

"Yes, do stay," he said and, looking at me, he repeated what he'd said in a persuasively firm voice, "Do stay."

Through the wide double window I could see the spacious recording studio and had a good view of the orchestra whose numbers seemed to have swelled in the meantime. I could also see the conductor's music-stand and the boom microphones looked like spindly cranes.

And there was the music-stand too at which Lemeshev and Tanya were standing side by side. Lemeshev bowed gallantly to Tanya, took off his jacket and hung it over the back of his chair, pulled down the knot of his tie and loosened his collar. All that made you realise he was about to get down to some really hard work. All he needed to complete the picture was to roll up his sleeves.

"Yakov Nasonovich, let's start off straight away without a run-through," came the voice of the conductor through the loudspeaker: "We'll go on the lines of yesterday's third rehearsal."

"Fine, I'm with you," answered the recording engineer.

The conductor raised his baton and the recording engineer pressed his button.

The spool started going round and I wondered

whether they were using a new reel of tape or that one on which my song had been recorded a moment ago. There had been lots of spare tape on it.... Why had they recorded my song after only one rehearsal when for these people there had been three whole rehearsals and, what's more, the day before the real thing.

I made ready to listen, but absolute silence reigned in the recording booth, although I could see that the conductor's baton had started swinging to and fro out there, the other side of the double window. The violinists were plying their bows, their cheeks pressed against their instruments, while the cellists with their knees wide apart had their eyes glued on their music and the harpists were plucking away at their strings.

But I couldn't hear anything; it was as if my ears had been blocked. I felt as if I was watching a silent film, when you see people running about, opening their mouths to scream, shooting pistols, without so much as a murmur.

I began to fidget on my chair and the recording engineer, without turning his head round, plugged another lead into the console and handed me some headphones, a reserve pair, I expect, because he was already wearing his.

And just in time it was, too, because the orchestral introduction was just drawing to a close. Then a woman's or rather a young girl's voice came in:

It was the nightingale and not the lark
That pierced the fearful hollow of thy ear...

and then a man's voice answered:

It was the lark, the herald of the morn,
No nightingale...

It was Romeo and Juliet. Juliet was assuring her beloved that it was not yet morning, for only the nightingale, the night singer, was trilling in the garden on the pomegranate tree. No, it was not morning yet, not yet time to part.

However Romeo was better at telling birds' voices than his love. He could hear that it was not the nightingale but the lark, and since it was the lark that meant morning, an end to their being together, time to part, otherwise he Romeo would not come out alive.

It was Tchaikovsky's music, his Romeo and Juliet duet, not from an opera but just a duet on its own. I knew that duet very well, I had heard it many times on the radio. Apart from being carried away by the actual music I admired something else as well, namely that Tchaikovsky had taken just one scene from that famous story, the balcony scene, and not even the whole scene itself but just the end of it, the parting. I must be honest and confess that I had not yet had time to read the story of Romeo and Juliet. I've meant to a hundred times but haven't got round to it all the same. But I knew the gist of it, the main outline. I knew all about the Montagues and the Capulets, that at the end everyone cuts each other to pieces or poisons each other—you couldn't avoid all that with Shakespeare! . . .

I felt grateful to Tchaikovsky for leaving to one side all those gory happenings and concentrating on the most important and the most beautiful thing—on love, Romeo and Juliet's love.

By now the roles had changed and Juliet herself, realising that morning has come and that the bird is no nightingale but indeed a lark, starts to beg Romeo to leave quickly, while he tried to convince her of the contrary, vowing that it is the nightingale. . . .

I'll say yon grey is not the morning's eye...

Two voices blending in perfect harmony, in a lover's plea.

I liked Tanya's voice very much, it was beautiful. Yet my attention was held more by another voice, Lemeshev's. There it was so close at hand and I hungrily caught every tone, every flexion. Every note held me spellbound, because that voice of Lemeshev's was a miracle that could not be put into words, a miracle of miracles.

Then came the final parting. . . . Romeo and Juliet tear themselves apart. . . .

Farewell, farewell...

That was all. Yakov Nasonovich took off his headphones and leant back in his chair. He wiped away the sweat from his bald head. He looked so tired, it was enough to make you think that it was he who had been conducting the orchestra and playing all the instruments, and singing both Romeo's and Juliet's parts, and even composed the music.

I took my headphones off as well. A smiling Tanya, a calm conductor and a worried Lemeshev came into the door. They sat down and waited for Yakov Nasonovich to wind back the tape. Now it was ready and there was a click, then a short pause and another click before the orchestral introduction.

By this time I was rather tired. I had been very worked up until my recording had been over and then there had come the unexpected appearance of the great singer followed by Tchaikovsky's music, which was impossible to just sit back and listen to without being carried away, without being deeply moved.

I have more care to stay than will to go
Come death and welcome! Juliet will it so.

In fact I was so tired I was no longer capable of following the voices or the orchestral accompaniment.

Some strange unconnected thoughts then started going round in my mind. I thought to myself that although they came to a sticky end Romeo and Juliet did have that one moment of overwhelming happiness, which perhaps is worth life itself.... And as I had heard that slip of a girl, Juliet, was only fourteen years old. Well, even I would be thirteen soon, and I of course wouldn't even make so bold as to dream of such rare passion. I was not even very sure whether anyone would ever love me, Zhenya Prokhorov, be it just for a short time. Yet I probably could love someone. I don't know who, but I think I might be able to, and make as good a job of it as Romeo....

Let me be ta'en, let me be put to death;
I am content, so thou wilt have it so.

"No, no, stop. Wait a minute!"

Lemeshev jumped up from his chair and waved his arms in protest.

"That won't do, it won't do at all!"

"What d'you mean, Sergei Yakovlevich? ..." asked the conductor shrugging his shoulders in surprise.

"But Sergei Yakovlevich..." exclaimed Tanya, pressing her hands to her heart.

"Hm-hm," said the recording engineer, clearing his throat and, turning back a sleeve of his white coat, he looked at his watch. It was probably time for him to go and have his lunch.

"It won't do. We must do it all over again!"

Without waiting for the others Lemeshev strode resolutely over to the door. Tanya and the conductor exchanged sighs and then meekly followed him. A few seconds later they came into view the other side of the wide double window inside the studio. Once more Lemeshev took off his jacket and hung it over the back of a chair.

"Good-bye," I said to the recording engineer. "Thank you."

"You're welcome," replied Yakov Nasonovich. "Good-bye."

I could see a barely disguised sneer in his eyes as if to say, you, my little friend, needed only one rehearsal, but dear Comrade Lemeshev finds four too few....

He was probably browned off at being made late for his lunch. I had not had mine yet either.

* * *

"What d'you mean 'run away'?"

"He's run away. Kolya Biryukov."

"How?"

"He's run away and that's all there is to it."

That stunning news was all round the school by the time I got back from the Recording Centre. Everyone knew all about it except me.

Back at the hostel there were boys clustering round one of the beds that looked exactly the same as all the dozens of others in the enormous dormitory. It was the bed which until that morning had been slept in by Nikolai Ivanovich Biryukov. Next to the bed there was a locker and somebody had opened it and left the door open so that everyone could see that it was empty. . . .

Kolya Biryukov had disappeared in broad daylight.

"Does Vladimir Konstantinovich know?"

"Yes. He came in here and has telephoned to the militia asking them to search for him."

Everyone was visibly upset by the unexpected event. Yet at the same time I was immediately aware of something else as well, timid admiration bordering on envy at the bold, secret get-away. . . . Any boy worthy of the name would have been attracted by the idea of such a feat.

"But I wonder where he went?" said Marat Aliev in wide-eyed astonishment. "Perhaps he went to the Caucasus, to the mountains?"

"What on earth would he want with your old Caucasus?" said Vitya Titarenko disparagingly. "You'll be suggesting a holiday resort next. Now I think he'll try and get to the Congo, to help Lumumba fight against the Whites."

"But Kolya himself is a white!"

"What?" said Vitya indignantly. "He's not a White, he's a Red. Get that into your thick head. It's not just a question of skin."

That put an end to the matter, Vitya's ingenuity had stunned us into silence.

"He won't make it," said Georgi Vyazemsky with a shake of his head. On hearing what had happened he had appeared at the hostel although he was a day-boy. "They'll stop him at the border, that's where they catch everyone. But anyway he won't even get as far as the border, how could he, without any money?"

On hearing that I bit my lip. It was only then that I grasped what must have happened. I began to see my recent visit with Kolya to the Bird Market in a new and quite different light—"Let's get out of here for a bit, Prokhorov", his "What for?" when I reminded him he had another two years to do at school, and his comment, "I don't like the way little fellows are being had." Yes, he had said all that at the Bird Market but there had been other things he must have kept to himself. And he had looked at me with an expression of wry pity as he might have looked at a baby. So he had already been planning to run away then, I suppose? Perhaps he had wanted me to go with him and put out feelers without being able to bring himself to come right out with it? Yes, of course, that was why he had shown me the dogs, for he knew that my life had been saved by a dog and that I dreamt of having a dog of my own. That was why he had gone up to the fellow with the shaven head to ask the price of his Alsatian. "So you think I can't pay for it? But I *can*!" And after that he had shown me the big wad of money. So that's what he was up to all the time!

I gave a quick pull at Georgi Vyazemsky's sleeve and winked to get him to follow me out into the corridor.

When we were outside Georgi asked: "Well, what is it?"

But I led him further away from the others right down the corridor to the washroom where I said to him:

"Listen, Georgi, but mind you don't go blurting this out to anyone, OK?"

"OK then."

"He did have money with him. I saw it with my own eyes.... A great pile of it."

"Where from?"

"His grant. He'd been saving a whole year. D'you get? You see he'd decided to do it as long ago as that."

Georgi turned his head to one side and didn't say anything for a bit while he thought over what I had just told him. Then, with unexpected abruptness, he said in a harsh tone: "Well, he did the right thing."

"What?" I said unbelievingly. "The right thing?"

"Yes."

In Georgi's eyes I caught the same gleam of unnerving superiority that my friend who had just staged his mysterious disappearing act had thrown in my direction at the Bird Market that time.

"I would run away myself—but it's out of the question for me. I've got parents here and they'd go out of their minds."

Georgi's gloomy face brightened all of a sudden and then he smiled and put his arm round my shoulder: "You see, it's like this. . . ."

4

"You see it's like this," said Georgi Vyazemsky. "My sister Maya has given instructions for me to invite you to her birthday party. You see, she's fallen for you, the old silly!"

Now when I think back to it, that conversation must have taken place later, nearer to the summer. Yes that's for sure—it must have been in May. Yes, definitely May, because I remember being rather surprised at the coincidence that a girl with the name of Maya should have been born in the month of May. It was only later that

 I realised I had got everything back to front, and that she had been called Maya precisely because she was born that month.

To cut a long story short it was that very same Maya who had made me feel such a fool in front of the packed Grand Hall of the Conservatoire by bringing me flowers and a note. There had been her telephone number in that note but of course I hadn't made use of it. I had been very sore at her.

But several months had passed since then and my anger had somehow subsided in the meantime. I didn't even try and get out of it when Georgi passed on her invitation to me.

"OK," I said, "I'll be there. But where d'you live?"

"Right close by on Begovaya Street."

As I had noticed before everything's within easy reach of our school, as if it had been made to order.

"Be there at six," said Georgi.

"All right."

When people are getting ready to go to a birthday party there are two problems to be solved—what to wear and what to take for a present.

The second problem presented no particular difficulties.

A month or two after my visit to the Recording Centre the composer had appeared at the school again; again I had been summoned to the director's study where the composer himself handed me three brand-new records. He took one of the records out of its sleeve and on the round label I caught sight of the words "Homing Signal", then came the name of the composer and underneath was written, "Sung by Yevgeni Prokhorov". His name was a fraction higher and mine a fraction lower but to all intents and purposes they were side by side on one and the same gramophone record.

The composer took a pen out of his pocket, thought for a moment and then wrote across the label, "To Zhenya Prokhorov with best wishes", and for a finishing touch came his flamboyant signature.

Of course I resolved there and then to keep that record with the dedication to the end of my days and never even put a needle to it, for the dedication made it something quite priceless. But the second record I took straight into the staff room and played it through a good hundred times without stopping. That's the one I still put on nowadays.

That meant that there was a third one left, which hadn't been touched and which was in a very attractive paper cover. Why not use that for Maya's present?

So in preparation for that party I took out the third record and when no one was around in the hostel I wrote on the label: "To Maya Vyazemskaya—with best wishes." I too rounded it off with an impressive signature.

It was just the cat's whiskers.

The second problem was a much more difficult and depressing business. What on earth should I wear? It was then that I first sensed acutely how wretched it was to have to live on institution food and to wear institution uniform all the time, for it meant you had everything laid on and yet you had nothing. There I was—fed, clothed and shod: what else did I need? Nothing. Then all of a sudden you're asked out to a birthday party and you discover you have nothing to go in. Of course I could have asked one of the matrons to let me have my concert get-up for one evening. Perhaps I would have got permission and she would have unlocked the cupboard to get it out for me. Yet in my heart of hearts I realised that to go along in that get-up would have been just as ridiculous as it would be for a conductor to turn up at a birthday party in tails, complete with piqué waistcoat, patent shoes and brandishing his baton—he would look a real fool of course.

So all that was still left open to me was to go along in my ordinary everyday school uniform made of plain grey material, with worn sleeves and trousers that bagged at the knees. At the party there were sure to be lots of Mummy's and Daddy's little darlings in fashionable little suits, imported sweaters and exotic tapered shoes. They'd be laughing at me behind my back, the wretches....

I was so fed up at the thought of it all that I was on the point of not going along. To hell with them and the birthday girl into the bargain. It was stupid of me to have gone and messed up the record.

And then a sudden wave of pride came over me. Not just ordinary common or garden pride but the professional pride of an artist. I remembered that all talented musicians worth their salt, that I had read about in books or heard stories about, always went about in shabby trousers, nibbled at dry bread, took shelter in garrets and hadn't got a sou to bless themselves with, yet they always had enough pride and self-respect to look down on empty-minded fops and, what's more, those very fops would court the musicians' favours....

After convincing myself of that I polished my shoes until they shone, tucked the record under my arm and set off for Begovaya Street.

* * *

My fears and worries vanished almost as soon as I set foot in the Vyazemskys' house.

No one paid any attention to my worn elbows and trousers bagging at the knees. My present was accepted by the birthday girl with such ecstatic delight that it was obvious, if anyone had presented her with the moon on a plate that day, it would have meant nothing to her beside my ordinary-looking gramophone record put out by the Aprelevsky Factory.

The programme for that birthday party was as follows—dancing, supper and then more dancing.

I won't go into details about the meal—it was a good birthday spread like any other.

Dancing ... was a rather difficult prospect because there were about fifteen of us fellows, boys to be precise, including me and Georgi, but there were only three girls; there were two apart from the birthday girl, a real pair of Ugly Sisters. I can't remember their real names, but only what they looked like and, believe me, they really were ugly.

Later when my wild love affair with Maya began I asked her one day why at that party there had been so many boys and only two girls, those Ugly Sisters. Maya then said to me quite honestly and without beating about the bush that she couldn't stand girls, she really hated them. She said that she had always made friends with boys and the whole baker's dozen of nice boys she had asked along to the party apart from Georgi and me had been boys from her class at school. She had been a close friend of every one of them at some stage of primary and later secondary school. They were all to that day of course still in love with her but she had long since got bored with them all. As for the two girls, Maya assured me that they were the only girls in the class worth having anything to do with: one was the Chairman of the Young Pioneer group and the other was editor of the class current events board. They were the only two for whom she was prepared to make an exception in her sweeping rejection of the female sex.

When it came to the point though neither the chairman nor the editor had any reason to regret their ill-fated looks that evening. They were in great demand, because the birthday girl Maya Vyazemskaya danced only with me.

We danced a whole lot of stupid dances—tangoes, foxtrots, the lot, because there was no twist in those days. Nowadays of course it's difficult to imagine that only a few years ago people managed to get along without it, could not have imagined it in their wildest dreams and didn't even know that they were standing on the threshold of that discovery and that in a couple of years' time the twist would suddenly appear and everybody would be dancing that gorgeous dance and finding it hard to grasp how no one had cottoned on to something as simple as that before, twirling the soles of one's feet and waggling one's hips to and fro?

Yet at that time people still hadn't got round to it and Maya and I danced all kinds of stupid dances like tangoes and the like, and while we danced them we looked at each other for after all it was the first time that we had seen each other close to. I don't know what kind of impression I made on her on closer examination. It must have been all right though. Otherwise she would never have danced with me the whole evening.

As for Maya, when I had a closer look, I thought she was very beautiful. I'd like to describe her beauty but I can't, because beauty, just like music, is quite impossible to put into words. It's not as if anyone would get an idea of what she looked like and be able to picture her if I merely described what kind of hair, eyes, nose and mouth she had. No one would be able to picture her and here's conclusive evidence: Maya Vyazemskaya was an exact copy of her brother Georgi Vyazemsky. There was only a year's difference between them which meant that Maya was a year younger than my school-friend and therefore a year younger than me too. Everything about them was the same: hair, eyes, noses and mouths. They were like two peas in a pod. And yet, believe it or not, Georgi Vyazemsky had a perfectly ordinary face: all you could tell when you looked at it was that his parents made him take vitamin pills every day and that the family used good quality soap.

But Maya Vyazemskaya, on the other hand, was as pretty as a picture even though she was the spit and image of him. Honest!

And then it turned out that brother Georgi was quite wrong to have called her an old silly. Maya turned out to be not just beautiful but intelligent as well. That became clear almost at once, when we started talking.

She came out with: "You know, you sang so well at that concert—it was really wonderful!"

I didn't protest.

"You know," she went on, "there's something really special about your voice. I'd never heard a voice like that before."

I didn't question that either. If she hadn't she hadn't.

"And it's not just me who thinks so," Maya insisted, although I didn't encourage her at all to go on about it. "Everyone thinks so. Mummy and Daddy and our friends. Everyone says that you have exceptional gifts, you see."

I nodded. Well, if everyone says so....

No, Georgi had been quite unjustly maligning his sister, when he called her a silly. Or at any rate he had been making a big mistake: Maya was a very intelligent girl and it was nice to know that her parents were also very intelligent people, and their friends as well....

Meanwhile I was itching to ask Maya a question myself. I had been thinking about it for a long time and had long been plucking up courage to put it to her. I wanted to ask her how she had known that evening of my début at the Conservatoire when she first saw me and heard me sing, how she could have known in advance that my voice would make such a big impression on her and that she'd take a fancy to me too? She couldn't have come along by chance with those flowers, could she now? Surely she hadn't been able to pick me out of the rows of boys in the choir beforehand? Or had she perhaps fallen for me sight unseen, after hearing stories from her brother Georgi?...

I was just about to ask Maya that question when her mother came into the room where we were dancing, clapped her hands and said in horror:

"Heavens, haven't you got bored of dancing yet? You've been doing nothing else ever since you all got here ... on and on. Surely you'd rather play a game or two?!"

"What though?" inquired the birthday girl. "Cards?"

"Football?" asked Georgi.

"Why on earth football?" exclaimed their mother in alarm. "There are perfectly harmless games for occasions like these. When I was your age we used to play forfeits for instance. . . ."

"Let's play forfeits," cried Maya.

"Like our forefathers did in the old days," added Georgi.

He brought out a blue velours hat from the hall and we all started putting our forfeits into its deep crown, all kinds of knick-knacks that we happened to have with us. One person put in a biro, another a handkerchief. One of the Ugly Sisters took off her watch and put that in and the other one used a brooch and as for me I had to use a comb: it was all I had with me because I hate going around with my pockets full of junk.

Maya installed herself on a chair and someone tied a scarf round her eyes so that she couldn't see. Georgi stood at the back of her chair and started to pull the forfeits out of the hat, one by one.

"What must the owner of this forfeit do?"

"Crow like a cock," commanded Maya in a firm tone.

One of the Ugly Sisters had to crow. She hesitated for a bit and then blushed, it was clear that she didn't like what she was being called on to do. After all she was the Chairman of the Young Pioneer group. Yet what could she do? There was no getting round it. It was just the luck of the draw, so up she'd have to get and crow.

She stood up on tiptoe and went: "Cock-a-doodle-do!"

Everyone clutched their sides. Georgi and I among them, their mother and the other Ugly Sister too. No one could contain themselves.

That is except for Maya who was sitting there with her eyes blindfolded, every inch the stern judge.

"And for this forfeit?" asked Georgi.

"A handstand."

A fat boy got up from the couch, he was the fattest and clumsiest of all the nice boys from Maya's class. He shrugged his shoulders helplessly.

"But . . . I can't."

"Do as you're told!" demanded Georgi. "What you can do is for the powers that be to decide."

Panting at the strain the fat little roly-poly put his hands down on the floor and tried to throw his legs up into the air. But his heavy heels kept on dropping back to the floor so that he had to start from the beginning again. He made a second attempt, and then a third. He tossed his legs up into the air like a little bull but in the end he just couldn't keep his balance and rolled over onto his side.

Once again everyone was laughing away.

"What must the owner of this forfeit do?" asked Georgi in a solemn voice. It looked to me as if he gave Maya's toe a quick nudge as he asked that time.

In an equally solemn voice Maya delivered her verdict: "Sing a song!"

My heart missed a beat. I assumed that Fate had been kind to me and I would have to sing, sing and not crow or do a handstand. I would have gladly sung. There was a piano on tap too and Georgi would probably have accompanied me. . . .

But Georgi was holding in his hand not my plastic comb but someone's biro. The owner of that object got up from his chair, scratched the top of his head looking rather bothered, and in a rather painful voice intoned:

I am a native of Vyatka,
Many a tear have I shed. . .

But at that moment the birthday girl tore the towel down from her eyes, jumped up and slapped her brother with it.

Later I was to learn that Maya had arranged with her brother in a hasty whisper when he tied the towel round her eyes that when my forfeit came out of the hat he would nudge her foot—making sure that no one noticed and that he didn't hurt her. Maya had also wanted me to have to do that particular forfeit. She had wanted to hear me sing again and for that she had been ready to break the iron rules of the game and resort to subterfuge, to cheating. Afterwards she told me the whole story.

But Georgi decided just for fun to pull a fast one on her and deliberately nudged her foot at the wrong moment. And it was for that that he got it in the neck.

Maya's face was ablaze with anger by this time.

"This is a ridiculous game," she declared, "and no wonder no one plays it nowadays! People should do what they know how to do and not what they haven't the faintest clue about."

She really was an exceptionally intelligent girl was Maya, and very beautiful too, even now when she was fuming with rage.

Her mother whose feelings had been hurt by the outburst sighed and left the room.

Maya then ran over to the record player and put on a new record. Again she and I started dancing. Once more I started plucking up courage to ask Maya how she had known in advance before the concert. In other words, why had she turned up there with flowers? But then all of a sudden I started to trip over my own feet, the strange indistinct music we were dancing to had me worried. From the other side of the room I looked over towards the spinning record.

"What is it? Don't you like it?" asked Maya in a concerned voice. "Don't you really like it? I like it very much. . . ."

"No," I said, feeling a bit awkward. "I do, but you see I think that records a 33 and it's been put on at 78."

"Really?" said Maya wide-eyed in astonishment. "I must have forgotten to change it over." And then she burst out laughing, "Never mind, let it play. To hell with it."

"To hell with it," I agreed.

"Let them go on dancing and we can run away."

"Where to?"

She pulled me by my sleeve and we slipped out of the door, then down a bit of corridor and through another door, and finally a third. At last we found ourselves on a balcony perched high above the city.

As I pointed out earlier it was May. The air

was full of a mixture of young buds and petrol and the lights had started to come on. At once I was able to find our local mountain of a building on Vosstaniye Square. It looked so near from where we were that you felt you could just stretch out a hand and touch it. A little further away were the sky-scraper on Smolenskaya Square, the Ukraina Hotel and the University. It was all spread out as if on the palm of your hand.

Right next to the balcony a fraction over to the right was a floodlit colonnade topped by four bronze horses rearing up into the sky. Behind them rose up a bronze charioteer pulling hard on the reins. If I had not already been an old Muscovite I would no doubt have thought that that was the Bolshoi Theatre. But I was an old Muscovite by then and I knew that the colonnade was not the one that belonged to the Bolshoi but the one in front of the racecourse. Admittedly I had never been to the races but I had some idea what they were like. Kolya Biryukov had explained to me that if you guessed which horse would come in first you could win money with no trouble at all. Kolya himself hadn't been to the races either but he had heard all about them from experts. The racecourse was a place where you could not only win piles of money but where you could also lose your last bean.

Yet from the outside it did look like the Bolshoi Theatre all the same. Even I an old Muscovite wanted to imagine to myself that the colonnade had nothing to do with the racecourse but was precisely the Bolshoi Theatre and that the rearing horses were the ones from the Bolshoi's quadriga that was familiar to people all over the world. Then the Bolshoi too would be a mere stone's throw away.

Maya and I stood there on the balcony without saying a word to each other. At last I had an opportunity to carry out my intention of asking her the question that had been plaguing me for so long. Why had she gone to the trouble of arming herself with a bouquet of daffodils before the concert?

I was working up to it, the words were on the tip of my tongue. But in the end I didn't manage to bring them out all the same. To be honest I was afraid to ask, heaven knows what kind of an answer she might have given me? Perhaps it would have been the very opposite of what I wanted to hear.

So we just stood there on the balcony, without saying anything to each other and yet I felt perfectly happy. The chariot drawn by four bronze horses reared up against the night sky.

By the way, on one occasion the whole school was taken to the Bolshoi Theatre to a matinee and at the very end of the performance real horses pranced onto the stage. I'm not kidding.

* * *

Soon after that I received three letters, all on the same day.

In the entrance hall of our school near the staircase there was a small table at which an old woman called Polina Romanovna used to sit. She wasn't a portress, nor a secretary. She was a kind of concierge I suppose, although that particular type of post has long ceased to exist. Polina Romanovna had been sitting there since the days when such posts *did* exist, when it used to be a general rule for some old woman to be seated in the entrance halls knitting and asking all those who came in who they were and why they might be there and whom they might intend to visit.

The following detail should make the picture quite clear: over the front door of the old building in which our school was housed—the building I keep meaning to devote proper space to, although I never seem to get that far—from the inside over the main door there used to hang a bronze bell. It was probably used long ago, when visitors would have used a bell-pull on the street side and it would have rung to herald their arrival. That was the way things were done in those days but that old custom had disappeared long since and electricity has come to take its place. Yet the bronze bell still hung over the door and thank goodness no one to this day has taken it into his head to dismantle the bell and take it to a scrap-dealer. Let it go on hanging there, it's never done anyone any harm.

Exactly the same thing applies to our concierge Polina Romanovna. She used to sit there at her little table, knitting away and asking strangers who they were, why they had come and watching to see that nobody played around too much on the stairs. And then when the post came she used to lay out the letters on her little table and some of the boys were even lucky enough to get money-orders too on occasions.

That table meant precious little to me though. There was nowhere for me to expect letters from, to say nothing of postal orders. So what? I just never used to look at the little table.

Then one wonderful day I flew into the hall, threw a greeting at the old woman in passing, ran over to the stairs when suddenly Polina Romanovna called over to me:

"Zhenya."

"Yes?"

"There's some post for you."

"What post?"

"Letters, three letters."

I retraced my steps to the little table, hardly able to believe my ears. Then I had a look and sure enough there were three letters lying on the table all addressed to me, to Prokhorov Zhenya. Of course I immediately started figuring out who was playing tricks on me. Our lot liked nothing better than a good leg-pull. However all the envelopes had genuine stamps stuck on them and postmarks in the right place.

Now that was a real surprise. In all my born days I had never received a letter and to be honest I hadn't ever let that worry me. Then all of a sudden, three at once. I still suspected that it was just some of the boys playing a joke on me and that on opening the envelopes I might find nothing inside, or a piece of paper with a skull and crossbones on it or something else equally stupid.

That made me decide not to open the letters at the next lesson and so rob the boys of a treat. I waited till the evening and then read them in a secluded corner of the building.

I've kept those letters to this day and I have reproduced them here in full.

The first letter:

Dear Zhenya,

It makes us all very happy to follow the progress you are making. Not long ago Rosa Mikhailovna told us that a song sung by you had been broadcast on the radio. Unfortunately none of us had heard the broadcast. Then we sent a joint letter to the Radio Committee asking them to broadcast your song again. We were informed that our request would be granted on the seventeenth of this month at half-past ten in the morning. At the appointed time we all gathered in the main hall and turned on the wireless set. At last the announcer said: "And now here's a request from children at the Lipetsk orphanage for pre-school children asking us to play the song 'Homing Signal' sung by Zhenya Prokhorov, a former inmate at the orphanage." We all held our breath as we listened to your song, Zhenya dear. Then we clapped you for a long time. At the moment all the children here are new since you were here and you wouldn't know any of them but nevertheless they know about you now and are proud of you.

We hope that when you become a professional singer you will come and visit us, come back to the home where you spent your early years.

Keep well and work hard at your studies.

Please convey my regards and heartfelt gratitude to Vladimir Konstantinovich.

Yours very sincerely,
Vera Ivanovna.

P.S. Warm regards to you from Rosa Mikhailovna too. At the moment she is teaching the children to sing "Homing Signal".

 The second letter:

Zhenya,

This letter comes to you from Sasha Tiunova from Lipetsk. You probably don't remember me—we were together at the orphanage in the same group. But I remember you very well although so many years have passed since then.

At the moment I am a Form VI pupil at a boarding school in Lipetsk. Sometimes we put on concerts here and after we have all done our piece we dance to the radiogram, but we have not got very many records here and have to dance to whatever we can get hold of. Well, yesterday someone brought along a new record. We put it on and I went to dance with Zina Gvozdeva (d'you remember her, she was also in our group?). Suddenly I realised that the voice on the record was very familiar but I couldn't think whose it was. When the music came to an end I went over to the radiogram and picked up the record to have a look.

When I saw your name on the record I nearly dropped it, I got such a shock. I put it on again although some of the others protested. You see, apart from Zina, no one would believe that I had known you since we were quite small. To this day no one will believe us!

Zhenya, if you can and if you have enough time what with all your lessons and concerts please write to me or Zina. A couple of words would do, just so that the other girls believe that we weren't telling enormous fibs.

And if you'd like to, do let's correspond. Incidentally I sometimes sing at our concerts here, although it's just for fun of course and all amateur stuff. Somebody has to do the singing!

So long,

Your former friend
Tiunova Sasha.

The third letter:

Zhenya,

It's me! How are you getting on? I'm jogging along OK. But don't you tell anyone anything for a bit. I'm specially not putting the sender's name and address on this envelope so that no one should find out where I am. To be brief I've found somewhere to live and I'm working on a fur farm, what as isn't important. We breed minks here, every colour under the sun: they're very fine, it's just a pity that afterwards they have to be sold abroad for foreign money, as if ours wasn't as good as theirs!

Zhenya, a search has been organised for me. It's V. K. trying to find me. The militia have been making inquiries, but the people here have been deliberately putting them off the scent because in a month's time I'll be sixteen and then no one will be able to force me to go back again. When the time comes I shall write to V. K. myself to ask him to send me my papers and the certificate I require to get my identity card issued.

The people here are very nice and understand everything. Zhenya, I've already got a dog of my own, a husky. He's called Pon, which means "dog" in Zyrian.

Don't try and write back yet, I deliberately haven't given you an address. But as soon as I get my papers in order then I'll give you all the details.

Are you still singing? Make the most of it while you can!

All the best.

K. B.

PART THREE

"Vitya! Vi-i-itya, come on!"

I was shouting my head off with all the rest, jumping up and down on the bench, although one might well have asked what the point was!

In the first place, he couldn't hear a thing although he was swimming without a cap on, because when you're swimming the crawl your ears are under water most of the time and in those short seconds when you turn your head to one side to gasp for air your ears are still full of water.

In the second place, when you're a mere fifty yards from the finishing line and has already covered three quarters of the distance I'm pretty sure that everything except your muscles and your heart must have been switched off for the time being as superfluous and that there was no time to see or listen for anything.

In the third place, there was no point in urging him on since no one else could hope to snatch his victory from him. At the very outset Vitya had got a six-foot start on all the other competitors and that gap had grown with every second, and now when Vitya was in the middle of the last length the others were all turning at the other end of the pool, their white heels glistening above the water....

But we went on shouting without a let-up, thankful that Nature had endowed us with such lusty throats and waving our arms about in the air. Because it was *our* Vitya, from our school, our Form VIII—Vitya Titarenko.

He won, and one after the other the umpires clicked their stop-watches shut and straightened up after crouching all that time at the end of the lanes. Then they all walked over to the umpires' table talking animatedly among themselves as they went.

And Vitya, as was expected of him, was floating about in the water to unwind and get his breath back. His rivals dived under the foam-rubber ropes between the lanes and swam over to him and there and then in the water they shook his hand, hugged him and slapped him on the shoulder demonstrating their sportsmanlike spirit: they were even up to that this young.

"Victory goes to Viktor Titarenko, of the Burevestnik Club," proclaimed the announcer. "His time was two minutes four seconds." Then he hesitated for a moment before adding, "Titarenko's time qualifies him for the Master of Sport title." Then came another pause and by this time it was obvious that he was quite at a loss and afraid to say the next bit. But out it had to come nevertheless: "Viktor Titarenko has set up a national record."

Great Scott! What started up in the stands after that would have woken the dead. Now not just us, Vitya's class-mates, but everybody else, people we didn't know, who had perhaps come from faraway, all started cheering, clapping and stamping their feet: quite a feat to set up a national record at fifteen and qualify to wear a coveted Master of Sport badge on your lapel! A mere fifteen!

The beaming coach threw a towelling wrap round Vitya's shoulders and led him away to the changing rooms.

"Shall we go and congratulate him?" asked an excited Georgi Vyazemsky.

"There's sure to be hundreds of people in there," I said hesitatingly.

 "So what?"

"And what if they don't let us in?"

"They'll let us in. After all he's our mate. Coming?"

"I'll go and see him afterwards back at the school."

"As you like."

As he ran off Georgi threw a mocking look at the two of us, at me and Maya. I was sitting next to her on one of the benches at the Luzhniki swimming pool. Maya had actually come along not with me but with her brother. We had arranged things in advance though and agreed that she would come. We had genuinely come along to cheer on Vitya and were sincerely thrilled at his triumph, but for us the most important thing was the meeting itself.

The summer was just over. The boys from our school had been sent to a Young Pioneer camp on the river Protva. But Maya had gone to the Crimea with her parents and then to one of the Valdai lakes, which were also a good distance away. Maya and I hadn't seen each other for nearly three months and it was already the second summer we had had to spend apart. To be honest the first summer after we started going out together I stood up to the separation fairly easily: I went swimming, fishing, mushroom-picking and enjoyed just loafing about doing nothing. There were times when I even forgot all about Maya's existence.

But this last summer had been quite different. It had dragged by unbearably slowly and what was more it had rained incessantly. I had read through lots of books and strummed away at the piano for want of anything better to do. And I had cursed myself for strictly forbidding Maya to write me letters, for fear that they would fall into someone's hands at the school, which would have made my life real murder.

However, I had held out bravely to the end of that second summer as well. And that day at the swimming competition we had met again at last. By now, though, I was quite convinced that I couldn't stand another summer apart.

Maya had come back from the Crimea and from the Valdai lakes looking quite a different person somehow. She had had her plaits cut off and her hair hardly covered the lobes of her ears. It only came down to the nape of her neck now and on top it was a deep gold. She was very sunburnt, but it wasn't those changes which had amazed me most of all. I had hardly recognised her after those last summer holidays: it was the Maya I had known before and yet it wasn't. She was no longer a little girl but a small and very attractive fourteen-year-old woman called Maya. I was struck dumb when I saw her.

As we sat there next to each other at the pool I realised that from now on I would have to see her every day otherwise I simply couldn't survive.

"Do you know," said Maya, "in Australia some girl has just set up a new world record, also in swimming. I read about it in *Komsomolskaya Pravda.* It said that it was not accidental either. Nowadays adults just can't keep up with children. That's why it's not just chance in Vitya's case either. Hot stuff, isn't it?"

"Yes, hot stuff," I agreed readily.

Everyone knows that love ennobles a man. I don't question it; it's true. Indeed very much so. But nevertheless I must confess a timid little thought that was taking shape in my mind at that moment: apart from the unquestionable ennobling effect, love can also make people behave rather shabbily. . . .

How could I have refused to go along with Georgi to the changing rooms and congratulate our friend Vitya Titarenko on his victory, his record-winning victory that qualified him for the Master of Sport title? It was horrible of me, really shabby. Yet I had done that horrible thing quite deliberately.

I had realised from the start that if I went to the changing rooms to congratulate Vitya then Maya would have to come with us, with Georgi and me (she couldn't have stayed behind by herself on the stands where there were lots of rough-looking types hanging around and drunks in groups of three sharing out bottles of vodka on the quiet). I had pictured to myself how, when we got to the changing rooms wreathed in smiles and cheering away, Maya, my Maya would see the brand-new champion and national record-holder Vitya Titarenko with his impressive physique and complete with victor's halo. . . . "Hallo Vitya, well done!" Maya would say and give him one of those smiles of which I hoped I had had a special monopoly for the last eighteen months. Then he, all shy and modest, would give a shrug of his sloping shoulders that betrayed the born swimmer and stretch out his whale of a hand. . . .

No, there's no doubt about it, love really does ennoble a man. But all the same I would rather have her stay behind on the stands talking to me and congratulate Vitya Titarenko later on.

"Who's for eskimo-pies, tubs or vanilla ice-creams?"

"Over here, please!" I called snapping my fingers to attract the ice-cream girl's attention.

I took some money out of my pocket. By then I was getting grant money and didn't need to ride on the trolley-bus without buying tickets any more and could even splash out for an occasional ice-cream. Only one though, for Maya. I couldn't have one; choir-boys' throats have to be taken proper care of.

"Thank you," said Maya, starting to lick away at her ice-cream. "It doesn't only apply to swimming either," she went on, "but to figure-skating as well. In that field children are coming out tops too—Schwarz, Kalma. . . . And as for gymnastics. . . ."

"Yeah," I said with a nod, hating all those precocious champions.

There were still four events to come, but now there was an intermission. Pop music came pouring out of the loudspeakers to jolly everyone along. I could feel it in my bones, I was quite sure that any moment I was going to come up against my worst and most threatening rival in the whole world. . . .

Sure enough there it came. . . .

Jama-ai-ai-ca! . . .

From that moment on the audience sat in hushed silence. I couldn't really say how the saliva glands of the esteemed audience would react to that very same "Jamaica" five or ten years later, how they would react to that voice that was ringing out over the stadium. I had no idea and wouldn't have liked to hazard a guess. But so far their conditioned reflexes were working most effectively. At the syllables "Jama-ai-ai-ca" their saliva started pouring in.

Even in my short life I have had the opportunity to observe similar cases of mass hysteria on a number of occasions. That happy-go-lucky fellow Yves Montand came over all the way from Paris and made all Moscow go weak at the knees. Van Cliburn threw audiences into raptures with either his playing or his hair-cut, and Yma Sumac from Peru had sent shivers up people's spines with her formidable portamentos, skipping over the octaves.

But that year was definitely the reign of Robertino, the Italian singer Robertino Loretti, who was the same age as I was.

Robertino was all the rage! He seemed to be the only thing people talked about. Everyone was frantically speculating as to when he would come to give concerts in the Soviet Union. From dawn to dusk it was Robertino Loretti's voice that could be heard in all the parks, cinemas, squares, stadiums, trains, river-steamers, bath-houses and hairdresser's. There were tremendous crushes whenever his records appeared on sale. People would walk along the streets squawking away like parrots: "O, pappagallo, pappagallo. . . ."

In short Moscow was gripped by some all-powerful hypnosis. I too of course had heard Robertino Loretti's songs and I liked the boy's voice. I had seen his photograph in magazines: he had dark eyes and hair, a bit like our Marat.

I swear, though, that I did not feel envious of him or experience any other violent feelings towards him. All I experienced was some bewilderment. After all, was my voice all that inferior to his? In recent months I had been doing a lot of solos at concerts and I had made a record too. Yet no one's ribs got broken in crushes to buy my record. Nobody printed my photograph in magazines and so far no one had invited me to go and give concerts in Italy. . . . Yet I repeat I had no real grudge against Robertino Loretti at all.

I saw in him a rival only in those rare moments when I was with Maya and then suddenly from out of nowhere his "Jama-ai-ai-ca" would ring out without any warning.

"He's going to Sweden," Maya told me.

I scowled and thought to myself he can go and jump in the lake for all cared.

With a hasty glance behind her Maya bent over as if she were about to whisper something into my ear but instead gave me a peck on the cheek. Her lips were as cold as ice after her eskimo-pie, or else my cheeks must have been so hot that they just seemed icy.

"It's all a load of poppycock," declared Maya.

"What is?"

"About people growing in height more rapidly than in intelligence, that really is poppycock. What do they set up specialised schools for, with a languages of maths bias. That's because they know it's important to start young, otherwise it'll be too late. You know there's one girl from our school—she left five years ago—and she got into the acting section of the Cinematography Institute. Now she's twenty-three though. She came to the school when a concert was being given and the girls asked her: 'What part d'you dream of playing?' She answered: 'I dreamt of playing Natasha Rostova, but it looks as though I'll have to do the old mother-in-law in Ostrovsky's *Thunderstorm.*' But what can you expect, she's twenty-three!"

That subject was Maya's hobby-horse at the time, she was always on about it. I didn't bother to argue with her.

Yet I couldn't work out what plans Maya herself had as regards her future. What would happen if suddenly three years later, as soon as she passed from school out into the big wide world, Maya should decide to get married? There was no doubt of course about whom she would be marrying: it would be me of course. Who else? Yet I was far from certain that by that time I would be able to lay on the vital wherewithal, whether I would have somewhere to live by then, a regular salary, saucepans, car and what not.

2

"Zhenya. Zhe-enya!"

I opened my eyes with an effort. It was in the afternoon after lessons. I had gone back to the hostel, taken my shoes off, flopped down on my bed and started reading Chernyshevsky's *What Is To Be Done*? which was our set text for literature lessons at the time. I'd already got through two of Vera Pavlovna's dreams and was about to start on the third when I fell asleep myself.

Then all of a sudden I was woken up by someone shaking my shoulder.

"Uh?"

Next to my bed was standing Usachov from Form III, an amusing little guy. He was very like me, like the boy I'd been when I had first been brought to the school a hundred years ago. He was a treble too and not a bad one at all. The whole of that summer he had never stopped shadowing me asking me stupid questions, which little midgets like that seem to have endless stores of. Then he would listen to every word of my replies with his mouth wide open. He by the way had the same name as me, he was another Zhenya, Zhenya Usachov.

And now here he was shaking me by the shoulder.

"Zhenya, wake up, Zhenya. . . ."

"What is it?"

"There's a man asking for you."

"Where?"

"Outside in the street by the gate."

"What kind of man?"

"We-ell. . ." He stuck out his chest, struck a pose and pursed his lips in a pout to show me what he was like.

"What does he want?"

"I don't know."

What a nuisance—a chap can't even be left alone to sleep in peace or to read a book.

I shoved my shoes on, patted my hair down with the palm of my hand and ran down the stairs.

By the gate to our hostel there actually was some character walking up and down, at a leisurely pace, looking very full of himself. I guessed at once that he must be the one, that little Zhenya had told me about. He really had a very imposing air about him, inflated with a sense of his own importance as it were. He was wearing a hard hat with a narrow brim a bit like a bowler, and in his mouth there was a cigar; that must have been what little Zhenya was trying to get across when he had pouted.

In other words it was clear he was the man. Slowing down a bit I walked up to him. But how would he recognise me? For no one would have described me to him.

However, the man in the hat on seeing me approach immediately gave me a smile, as if I was an old friend. He must have recognised me then.

 Well there was nothing surprising about that I suppose: he had probably seen me at a concert or on the television programme we had been on earlier that month.

He held out a flabby hand in my direction:

"Hallo. I'm Viktor Viktorovich."

"Er-er, hullo," I replied.

(In all my born days I had never seen or heard of any Viktor Viktorovich.)

"Let's walk along together for a bit," he suggested.

"Why not," I agreed.

We started walking in the direction of bustling Presnya Street, but not in the direction of the school building but the opposite one and then turned down into a quiet side-street.

Viktor Viktorovich threw his cigar-butt into a nearby litter-bin.

"Zhenya," he said, "do you know that art belongs to the people?"

"Yes," I replied, "who else?"

"Quite right," went on Viktor Viktorovich. "It belongs to the people, to the masses. Don't you agree?"

"Of course."

"And do you know that the artist is duty-bound to bring his art to the masses, to satisfy their cultural needs?"

"Yes," I agreed again. "Only couldn't you get to the point?"

"That's what I like to hear," he said laughing. "What are you doing tomorrow evening? Are you free?"

"Yes," I said. "Well, I've got some homework to do, but nothing really important."

"O-ho, that'll never do!" said Viktor Viktorovich with a disapproving shake of the head.

"You'll have to get your homework finished early and at 17:00 you must be standing out here on the corner. Are you with me? A mini-bus will drive up and I'll be in it and then off we go."

"But where to?" I asked, feeling quite curious about it all by this time.

"To the people, to the masses. Not far, a mere twenty-five miles. We'll be back by twelve. Any objections?"

"I personally don't have any," I said. "But I'm afraid you'll have to see the director about it and arrange things with him. If Vladimir Konstantinovich says it's OK then I'm game."

Viktor Viktorovich stopped in his tracks, put his hand inside his jacket, brought out a new cigar, bit off the end and spat it out, lit it with his lighter and screwed up his eyes disparagingly.

"Hm-mm, well!" said Viktor Viktorovich with undisguised pity. "And I thought I was dealing with an adult!"

"Not a hope," I said with a sigh. "We're still small fry and foolish."

"I can see that now."

I did an about-turn and strode away from him.

"Zhenya! Wait a minute!"

He caught up with me, panting in an agitated way.

"Now why did you have to go and get worked up like that? Let's talk this over seriously. I want you to realise that. . . ."

Realise what? I'd cottoned on long since. From the moment I saw him, from the moment he opened his mouth.

I'd realised straight away that that Viktor Viktorovich was trying to rope me in for some shady deal . . . although he was wearing a fashionable hat, and smoking an imported cigar. A fat lot that meant! Any fool knows that you can buy dear cigars at fairly low prices here and that any cool cat can smoke the same kind of cigars as Ford, Rolls Royce or whoever.

In short I had seen right from the start that I was up against a nasty piece of work, one of those people whose doings are eventually exposed in the press. Nor did my intuition let me down. Exactly, a year after that Viktor Viktorovich got first into the papers and then the nick. Thank goodness that by that time I was having nothing more to do with him. It would have been better off if I had never had anything to do with him in the first place.

But for the moment we were still standing there having confidential chat in the quiet side-street near Presnya.

"Let's talk things over seriously," repeated Viktor Viktorovich. "I want you to understand. Now, tell me, why do you think all one hears everywhere nowadays is that Lobertino fellow."

"Robertino," I corrected him.

"Yes, well you know who I mean, the Loretti fellow. Wherever you turn, now, why? Why is it that there's all this worship of things foreign here, eh?"

I shrugged my shoulders to show I didn't know. And indeed why was there?

"It's not as if there's no one here in Russia with a decent voice, now is it?" he went on in an indignant tone. "There's plenty of talent now, isn't there? Surely we could find our own Lobertino?"

"Robertino," I corrected him again, finding it annoying by this time.

He sure was thick that fellow. He couldn't pronounce the name properly despite his fine hat and cigar. And although he was of course an out-and-out crook he probably had some kind of connection with the art world, at least indirectly, seeing that he was discussing things like this with me out there. Pity though it is, among people connected with the world of art you do sometimes come across types who are really thick. In their own particular sphere they may be most competent, when it comes to playing the violin or the trumpet for instance, indeed they may be excellent players: but let them so much as open their mouths, and—strike me pink, it sets your teeth on edge. And at that moment I was getting very annoyed with Viktor Viktorovich and his Lobertino! I ask you!

I found this particularly annoying since at the same time I agreed with quite a lot of what he had to say. After all why did people worship anything from abroad so much? Robertino, Robertino, Robertino . . . as if nothing else counted at all!

"Zhenya," said Viktor Viktorovich, who had probably noticed by that time that I was starting to come round. "What are you worrying your head about now? You won't be the only person performing. We've got a whole concert troupe, but *you'll* be the star attraction!"

Yes, it really was glaringly unfair. Anyone would think that here in Russia there was no one who could sing, that there was no talent! In our school alone there was a fair number of voices with a better tone than Robertino's.

"Zhenya," said Viktor Viktorovich, "you'll get twenty rubles for each performance. Let's say ten concerts to begin with."

Yes, I was sure that at our school there were at least twenty voices of the same standard as Robertino Loretti's. And that was from among a mere two hundred boys.

"So we meet tomorrow then," said Viktor Viktorovich.

"What time?"

"At 17:00 hours, at that corner over there, d'you see where I mean?"

"Yes."

"A mini-bus will drive up."

He looked me up and down in a business-like way and said: "Well, as for clothes, we'll look something out for you and later you'll be able to buy your own. You'd better give us something of Lobertino's. . . ."

"Robertino's."

"Yes, yes something of Loretti's. That's what the audience wants. . . . You know how it is. . . ."

Of course I knew all those songs about Jamaica and parrots and the like, I knew every note and intonation. As I pointed out earlier, ever since I was a little kid, I've been able to pick up tunes at first hearing. And since then think of all the training we'd had. But what would I do for words?

"I don't know the words," I told him.

"I've seen to that too," said Viktor Viktorovich with an efficient nod. Then he brought some papers out of his pocket on which someone had written out the words.

"Can you make out that lot?"

"But, it's in Italian!"

"Of course it is. Real Italian. What else did you expect?"

"I don't know Italian, we learn German."

"Why?"

Who knows why? I myself had asked that question too. After all everybody knew that musicians ought to learn Italian. Probably it had just been difficult to find an Italian teacher.

Viktor Viktorovich stood there turning over the

pieces of paper with a rather worried expression on his face. He frowned and said: "But the letters are the same surely? They're foreign letters, what difference does it make?"

"Foreign letters" indeed. What an oaf!

"All right," I said, taking the pieces of paper.

"17:00 hours," Viktor Viktorovich reminded me before we went our separate ways.

"I'll be there."

* * *

"Till tomorrow then," he had said. All that was left till then was just over twenty-four hours. I still had time to think things over, to chew over the pros and cons, let my conscience come into play and weight things up properly. I thought to myself how he would run round in circles on that corner waiting for me with the mini-bus and with his ridiculous cigars. I might even hide round the corner and giggle at him. Or I could take another of our boys along with me, say Georgi Vyazemsky, to get a kick out of it all. The sight would surely make anyone die from laughing!

Things didn't turn out a bit like that though. There was no laughing, no chewing over the pros and cons. To be more precise I just can't bring myself to tell how my conscience plagued me, how it kept me awake the whole of that night. I just can't, I don't want to start justifying myself, because people never justify themselves to make other people pity them, but so as to indulge in self-pity: oh, what a poor unfortunate chap I was. . . .

But I'm not going to sink to that, particularly as it's all old hat now, something that belongs to the past. It wasn't because of myself that I couldn't sleep that night but because of our director Vladimir Konstantinovich. The point was that not long before that unfortunate meeting of mine with Viktor Viktorovich a militia-man had come round to the school, a smart young sergeant. He was in the director's study all of two hours. And all that time they were alone, just the two of them. However we all knew what was being discussed.

It was Kolya Biryukov! The militia had managed to find him in the end, in the idyllic place where he was hiding. But fortunately by that time he had had his sixteenth birthday. Now he was a fully-fledged citizen who couldn't simply be picked up by the scruff of his neck and carried off home. In fact the militia-man had only really come to see Vladimir Konstantinovich to make sure that Kolya's papers were sent off to the place where he was now living, so that his identity card could be made out. (Things had turned out exactly as he had said they would, it had all gone according to plan. There was a chap for you—good old Nikolai Ivanovich!)

However, that subject would not have been enough to keep them at it for two whole hours, five minutes would have done, yet they had been sitting talking for two hours. I had it on good authority that Kolya's papers were not the only thing they discussed. The militia-man put out careful feelers to find out what measures might best be taken to ensure that no other boys ran away anywhere and then have to be searched for the length and breadth of the Soviet Union. The director had replied saying that the incident with Biryukov was the exception, not the rule, the result of emotional stress. Then the militia-man inquired politely whether measures couldn't be taken in the future to ensure that such emotional stress did not recur, or to see that the boys didn't lose their voices? At that Vladimir Konstantinovich lost his temper and even started shouting, declaring that he was not the God Almighty or Mother Nature, otherwise he would long since have put things to rights.

That would have been the end of the matter and probably no one would have heard anything about the whole discussion if the smart sergeant hadn't gone on to ask Vladimir Konstantinovich in a shy, rather awkward manner if he would listen to his voice. He had been told, he went on, that he had an operatic tenor and he had been taking part in militia concerts, so could the professor be so kind as to tell him his opinion of his singing potential?

This detail of the conversation was soon common knowledge and not merely thanks to rumours, for we were all able to hear the sergeant singing Lensky's aria from Tchaikovsky's "Eugene Onegin". Afterwards we all saw him leaving the building with his face wreathed in smiles.

But after that visit Vladimir Konstantinovich had to take to his bed immediately. He had had trouble with his liver before but this time it was a serious bout and after the conversation with the sergeant he had to spend six weeks in hospital.

That was why I had not been able to get to sleep the whole night. I had been thinking about Vladimir Konstantinovich, or rather how he would have reacted to Viktor Viktorovich. I was thinking about what our old director would have said if he got to know about the meeting planned for the next day at 17:00 hours. That was what made me toss about in my bed all night unable to go to sleep.

But the next morning I got up feeling perfectly fresh as if nothing had been bothering me in the slightest. My head was clear and so light on my shoulders that you might have thought it was quite empty.

3

I was the star attraction and that was why I was kept back to the end. That meant that I had the pleasure of standing in the wings and watching the whole programme, the whole "Grand Concert by Well-Known Moscow Artistes" as it was called on the plywood placard that had been put up at the door of the state-farm club-house.

The club-house was small, and so were the hall and the stage. But the farm as far as I could gather was not small as the small hall was crammed fit to burst. They all seemed to have come along, the men and the women, young and old. They had all been drawn along at the prospect of the "Grand Concert". It looked as if no well-known Moscow artistes had been near that particular state farm for some time. Viktor Viktorovich who was in charge of the show obviously knew just the places to take his "pirate" troupe to. It seemed very much as if this particular club had not seen a concert for donkey's years, of either the "pirate" or the official variety. You could tell that from the appreciative enthusiasm with which the audience greeted each item.

When the mini-bus drove up to the appointed corner at five o'clock sharp and I clambered in, I greeted the assembled company and looking round noticed that even counting me and the driver there were only eight people in the mini-bus. Even before we got there I started thinking to myself: will that be enough to lay on a full-scale concert? After reading the placard at the entrance I felt still more uneasy about the whole business. Only seven of us, because the driver didn't count, and a Grand Concert? . . .

But as it turned out I had underestimated the potential of our Magnificent Seven. Take Viktor Viktorovich himself for one. In the beginning I had thought that he was nothing but a go-getter and rogue, who made a habit of organising "pirate" concerts and making a tidy packet for himself out of it. But he turned out to be quite a star in his own right, a compère of the first order! He was the first to appear on the stage and he started telling the audience all sorts of funny stories, which I for one knew since third-form days and had read later in old copies of the magazine *Crocodile*. It was more than likely that the people sitting out there in the hall had heard those jokes before, stories about floor polishers and militiamen, cashiers and shop assistants, Adenauer and Eisenhower; after all, they, too, were bound to have gone through school and to have looked at the occasional magazine.

However, Viktor Viktorovich with no hesitation at all introduced something of himself, his own personal variations into those stale funny stories. He made them sound as if they had all befallen himself or his close friends. His tone seemed so utterly sincere that you couldn't possibly question his integrity. It seemed perfectly natural to everybody—myself included—that he Viktor Viktorovich, no other, had had dealings with floor polishers and shop assistants, associated with cashiers and militia-men and that his close friends had rubbed elbows with Eisenhower.

The audience was laughing merrily away in no time at all and soon afterwards Viktor Viktorovich announced the next item. The next performers were two acrobats, a man and a woman. And I must say they put on a very original act. At any rate I have never seen a pair of acrobats to beat them, either before or since.

Even before they went out front, when they donned their costumes—hers was white and decorated with sequins and his was black and also decorated with sequins—I remember my mind boggling at the thought of what might follow. You see, she was a tall young blonde with broad shoulders and massive legs, while he was a whole head shorter, bony and frail-looking, though wiry, and believe it or not, pushing fifty by the looks of it. From close-to it was obvious that his hair was really grey and dyed black to match his costume, and hers incidentally was also dyed blonde to go better with her costume.

I couldn't possibly imagine how the poor puny character would be able to lift the hefty wench even an inch off the floor.

But that in fact was the whole point of the act. As soon as they had run out on to the stage, she —the woman!—with one sweep of her arms perched her partner on her shoulders.

The audience was spellbound.

Then tensing up her muscles a bit she—the woman!—threw him up into a handstand on her head.

The onlookers gasped with amazement.

Then he balanced on her head with one hand, leaving go with the other, and slowly swung his legs out to one side.

A storm of applause broke out.

What followed defies description. What that Amazon creature did with her partner was just nobody's business. She threw him into the air and caught him as he hurtled down. She swung him round by his arms. She twisted him round in circles, tied him up in knots, she curled him up in a ball and then sent him soaring through the air like a boomerang.

The more weird and wonderful things she did with him, the more ecstatic the audience grew. I must confess that by that time I was beginning to feel a little shaky at the knees. I was starting to worry that my turn would be a come-down after them: could I hope possibly to keep up. I started to doubt whether I really would be the "star attraction".

But the items that followed, including all Viktor Viktorovich's stupid chatter, bucked me up a bit, for they were definitely on the seedy side.

There was a xylophone solo and then conjuring tricks. Neither item was really worth mentioning, all the old stuff that you see in any variety programme, that is with the exception of two things which are well worth describing.

The xylophone solo was just a xylophone solo. A man walked on stage in a black suit, picked up two little hammers and started to give us a Strauss pot-pourri. He played his piece, bowed to the audience and walked off. That was all there was to it. Yet that xylophonist in the black suit was dead drunk.

In the mini-bus on the way there I had noticed that he kept bringing a flat flask out of his pocket and taking a swig, giving a shudder as it went down and then smacking his lips in satisfaction and stowing the flask back into his pocket. His eyes were quite bleary even then and he'd started muttering unintelligible rubbish to himself.

I had felt like suggesting to Viktor Viktorovich that he shouldn't let the xylophonist go out on stage, since he was dead drunk and might well make a fool of himself out there in front of the audience and disrupt the whole concert. But I was held back by the thought that after all Viktor Viktorovich was bound to know the player better than I did and that he, too, must have noticed the flask and there was no point in my poking my nose into the whole business. It turned out that I had made the right decision.

You see, as soon as the xylophone solo had been announced, the man in the black suit straightened up, walked out on to the stage with firm strides, picked up his hammers and started playing the Strauss pot-pourri like a real virtuoso, confidently without even the tiniest slip. Then he replaced the little hammers in their case, took his bow and retired.

Once again I had an example before me of how important training and professionalism are in the work of us artists.

The conjuror was sober though. He performed all his mystifying tricks in full view of the audience and even I, standing there in the wings, slightly behind and to one side of him, was unable to grasp how he did them and to probe his secrets. Say what you will, it's not the tricks themselves that draw the crowds but the chance of seeing through the sleight of hand and being able to point at the conjuror and say: "Well, my friend, we've caught you out this time!"

But there was no seeing through Viktor Viktorovich's conjuror. He tore pieces of newspaper into shreads, crumpled them up, rolled them all up together in a ball and then carefully unfolded the whole caboodle—and behold, the newspaper was whole again. Out of his top-hat he pulled handkerchiefs, a pile of different coloured ribbons, bouquets of flowers and topped it all by a great big hen. Not only did I fail to notice how it got into the empty top-hat but it was also beyond me how I had overlooked the noisy hen on the way in the mini-bus. I could have sworn that no chick had been travelling with us. Mercy me!

Yet the most fantastic of all his turns was the trick with money. The conjuror pulled down his shirt cuff, raised his arm and started to move his fingers. One shake and a red ten-ruble note appeared, another and out came a second ten-ruble note. The notes came tumbling out, one after the other, and one by one he stowed them away in his pocket. All the time he never stopped smiling as they came out, ten rubles, ten rubles, and yet another ten. . . .

I don't really know whether that trick with the money was the most complicated of all—perhaps pulling the hen out of the empty top hat was a more formidable feat—yet it was quite clear that it was the red ten-ruble notes that made the biggest impact on the audience, conjured up as they were from nowhere, from out of thin air, without the slightest trouble at all—one flick of the fingers, and there you were with ten whole rubles!

To be fair, I shouldn't leave Asya out, the last member of our Magnificent Seven. She was the pianist and throughout the whole show she never once got up from the piano stool and stayed put all the time at the rickety old club piano. She gave us a rousing march when the curtain first rose. It was she that accompanied the pair of acrobats and then the conjuror with his hen and last of all it was her turn to accompany me. Asya was an old lady close on a hundred, yet everyone still called her by her first name as if she were a little girl. I never managed to discover her full name and when I used to talk to her I always avoided calling her anything. Before the concert started, when the curtain was still down, Asya and I had a quick run-through: I was singing falsetto under my breath and right away she started fitting in the accompaniment and when the time came we were sure of each other. I was positive right from the start that Asya would never, let me down.

Viktor Viktorovich walked to the centre of the stage, came out with yet another funny story to jolly up the audience and then puffing out his chest he proclaimed proudly: "And now you shall hear Zhenya Prokhorov! Our own Lobertino Loretti!"

What a let-down! Yet out there in the audience it looked as if people had failed to catch his shameful mistake or chosen to ignore it, so thrilled were they at the news, that there existed on our planet another Robertino and, what's more, a home-grown Soviet one, whom they were going to see and hear that very instant.

Go on, then, look and listen. Here I come, Zhenya Prokhorov.

Sul mare luccica
L'astro d'argento...

I wasn't worried that my actual singing wouldn't be good enough. I knew that I was singing well. That was something I was used to. It was something else that made me feel uneasy. The whole evening I had been swotting off those Neapolitan songs. I had been learning words whose meaning I couldn't understand but only guess at. What difference did it make though, what they meant? The main thing was to pronounce them properly and not make a fool of myself like Viktor Viktorovich with his ridiculous "Lobertino". But it was precisely that that had me worried: was I pronouncing them right? After all, they were Italian and I was reading them as if they were German words and pronouncing them Russian style. God alone knows, perhaps there *were* some special secrets I ought to have mastered, just like the ones peculiar to German and Russian, like the way the Germans write words one way and pronounce them another for instance. The English, so I've heard, go one further (Maya told me and she learnt English at school) and read Liverpool when they write Manchester! Could I really be sure in that case that I was doing justice to all the "l'astro's" and "d'argento's"?

Yet I took considerable comfort from the assumption that out there in the audience there would hardly be many linguists who were in a position to pick out my pronunciation slips.

I also took heart from consideration that whatever might go for the rest, there were two words that I had definitely got right, two of the most important words in the song, two words that come in the triumphant refrain:

Santa Lucia,
Santa Lu-u-ucia!...

Viktor Viktorovich had been right after all. My number did turn out to be the star attraction. Nobody, not the acrobats, not the conjuror, no one was given the applause that I got: there was no end to it. At first they clapped in the usual fashion and later when their palms were sore they started clapping as people do nowadays all together in friendly unison, insistently asking for more, more, mo-o-ore!

But what could we give them after that? Asya and I had arranged in advance that we would do just three songs. The other ones that I knew Asya didn't know and the ones that Asya might have known I didn't know. Yet the audience went on demanding more and more!

So I had to go on and on repeating one and the same thing:

O dolce Napoli,
O suol beato...

Then again they started chanting: "Santa Lucia! Santa Lucia!"

And as I kept on taking bows one after the other I stopped reproaching myself for succumbing to Viktor Viktorovich's persuasion tactics, breaking school rules and going on a secret trip to the state-farm club.

It would have been better still, of course, if there hadn't had to be all that secrecy about the whole affair and it would have been a lot nicer without Viktor Viktorovich.

Whose fault was it, though, that those kind, big-hearted, hospitable people in that state farm, not so far from Moscow, after all never had a chance to see any but "pirate" concerts organised by crooks like Viktor Viktorovich.

* * *

Only twenty-five miles but the return journey was done in the dark and it seemed endless.

I had taken a seat at the back of the mini-bus

and was sitting huddled in a corner. I was very tired and couldn't help dozing off. I kept on waking up and then falling asleep again. There seemed to be no end to the journey.

At one stage I woke up and saw a strip of concrete coming towards us, lit up by the headlights. Thick pine trees bordered the concrete on both sides.

Out I went again only to see the concrete coming towards us and the black pine trees looming up at the side of the road when I woke up.

Each time I woke up it was the same—darkness, concrete, pine trees.

4

"Ah-a-ah."

"All right. Next one, please."

"Ah-a-ah. . . ."

"All right, Usachov. You can go now. Next one, please."

It was a Monday, the day when the whole school, every boy from every class, had to go through that medical inspection or rather be looked at by the ears-nose-and-throat doctor, dear old Maria Leontyevna.

"Aliev! Take a seat, sonny."

"Ah-a-ah."

"Once more, please."

"Ah-a-ah."

"Well, well. That's interesting."

"What is it?" asked Marat Aliev, his dark eyes full of concern and his piece of lint still hanging on to the end of his tongue.

"There's nothing to worry about yet," said Maria Leontyevna with a quick but highly significant glance in the direction of Vladimir Konstantinovich who was sitting next to her.

"You can go now, Marat. Next, please."

"Ah-a-ah. . . ."

"All right, next one, please."

"Morning, Maria Leontyevna."

"Morning, Zhenya. Well now, open up."

The dazzling yellow light that bounced off the round mirror attached to her forehead made me blink. I felt the familiar cold metal of the laryngoscope on the back of my tongue.

"Ah-a-ah."

"Once more, please."

"Ah-a-ah."

"Once more."

"Ah-a-ah."

"That'll be all."

Maria Leontyevna put the metal instrument back on the tray with a clank and, with a slight movement of her hand, she pushed the mirror up out of the way.

"Well, Zhenya. You'll have to give the singing a miss for the time being. You've got to give those chords a rest. Chords like yours are worth looking after. You do see, don't you?"

She was looking down at me with a calm kind expression on her face. But I felt my tongue and my throat suddenly go dry, and drops of sweat break out on my forehead. But I didn't say anything.

"Vladimir Konstantinovich," said the doctor still with that calm gentle expression on her face, "Prokhorov mustn't do any singing. Are there to be any concerts in the near future?"

"No, not for the moment. We're working on a new programme. We-ell, if he mustn't, I suppose he mustn't."

With a concentrated look on his face Vladimir Konstantinovich started wiping his glasses on his handkerchief. It looked as if he had been put out a bit by the news. Although he must have realised that sooner or later it would have had to come. All the same, he still seemed put out by it. That was most likely why he put his glasses back on his nose in such a decisive way and went on in a harsh tone:

"If he mustn't, then he mustn't. By the way, Zhenya, haven't you been getting bad marks in geometry recently?"

I didn't say anything, I simply couldn't talk at all. I was struck dumb by it all.

"You've been getting bad marks in geometry," repeated the director. "You'd better pull your socks up my lad."

"Next one, please," said Maria Leontyevna.

But I was still sitting in the chair. I couldn't move a limb.

"It's silly of you to get upset like that, Zhenya," she chided leaning down towards me and talking in a low voice. "It's perfectly natural. It's just a question of age. You're growing up and you must behave like a real man. Go on with you now."

Then she raised her voice and said, "Next one, please."

"Ah-a-ah."

"Fine. That's quite all right. Next one, please."

"Ah-a-ah. . . ."

* * *

We met as arranged after school in the same side-street. "It's to be at the Metalworkers' Palace of Culture!" Viktor Viktorovich announced beaming away. "It's only just been completed. It seats a thousand and the acoustics . . . wow!"

"Viktor Viktorovich. . . ."

"The posters are being done now. It starts at 19:00. It takes an hour to get there from here, so that means we'll have to pick you up. . . ."

"Viktor Viktorovich. . . ."

"What is it? Oh, I nearly forgot: I still owe you . . ." with that he put his hand inside his jacket, still all smiles.

"Viktor Viktorovich, I'm not coming."

"What?" His eyebrows shot up and the hand that he'd put into his jacket pocket froze there. "What d'you mean, you're not coming?"

"I can't come."

"What d'you mean—you can't? The posters are being put up and the tickets are being sold. What nonsense are you on about?"

"It's not nonsense. I'm serious: I can't come."

"But why, for Heaven's sake?"

He gave an indignant snort.

I looked down at my feet. I felt rather awkward and ashamed of myself. I was well aware I was letting him down terribly, old Viktor Viktorovich. OK, so he was a bit short on grey matter and probably a crook into the bargain, but he was human after all. He was always rushing about in a frenzy arranging things and here I was doing the dirty on him. I felt very ashamed, knowing how much I was letting him down.

"Zhenya, what's the matter?"

"I mustn't do any singing."

"What d'you mean 'mustn't'?"

"I just mustn't. Doctor's orders. But it's not for good, just for the time being," I went on hurrying to reassure him.

"O-oh, so that's it!" The arm that had got stuck in his inside pocket came to life again: he brought out a cigar, then came the click of his lighter and the first puff of grey smoke.

"O-oh, so that's it," he repeated in a thoughtful tone.

"Yes," I went on with a nod. "Just for the time being. Perhaps it won't be for very long. In some cases it's not for long at all."

"So you've had it?"

"What d'you mean?" I didn't grasp what he was getting at.

"You've had it," he repeated. This time the words were not a question though. There was no note of inquiry in his voice any more. He wasn't asking a question, just stating a fact.

"What d'you mean, I've had it?" I asked in surprise once more.

I was really at sea: the daft fellow and I were carrying on a quite unintelligible and stupid conversation.

"Yes, Zhenya. You've had it and that's all there is to it."

He said that gazing down at me with a cruel look of undisguised pity.

It was only then that it hit me what he was on about.

I screamed back at him: "No!" We had been standing talking in the side-street near Presnya. It was a fairly quiet spot, not like Presnya itself which was always full of bustling crowds and the rattle and bang of traffic. It was quiet and fairly deserted, not that there wasn't a living soul to be seen there though. There was an old woman going past carrying a big shopping bag, and walking in the opposite direction there were two small girls, probably going to the Zoo. A little further off there was a Volga car with its bonnet up and a driver bending down underneath, rummaging about in the engine.

But for the main things were quiet, and I rent that quiet by screaming at the top of my voice.

"No-o-o!!!"

At that moment everything seemed to go dark in front of me, yet somehow I still managed to see how a ginger cat made a dash for an open gateway terrified out of its wits, how a tousled head emerged from the Volga bonnet, how the old granny with the shopping bag looked round and the two small girls on their way to the Zoo started to giggle.

Viktor Viktorovich peered round in alarm and scowled.

"Come off it!" he muttered. "Come along now. . . ."

"When is it?" I asked.

"When's what?"

"When am I going to be picked up?" I asked standing there with my fists clenched so tightly that my nails were cutting into my palms.

"Can you make it then?" You could see a flash of hope lighting up the gloomy doubt on his face by that time. What I would have given to bash his face in at that moment!

"When is it?"

"Tomorrow at half past five, here, at the usual place."

"All right, I'll be there. Good-bye."

"Zhenya, wait a moment." Once more he started rummaging around in his inside pocket. "Here's some more. . . ."

But I just turned away and strode back to the hostel, without looking back at him.

"Our own Robertino Loretti!"

At last he'd got it. For the first time he'd managed to pronounce that name right. Well at least I'd been able to teach him that much.

After that came the odd buzz and squeak as he lowered the microphone, adjusting it for me.

Now I had to come out and do the act he had trained me for. I came out on stage from the wings, smiling shyly and naively, pretending to be dazzled by the bright light of the projectors and the half-hearted applause. I walked up to the microphone, peered at it from first one side and then the other, tapped the mesh with my finger, shrugged my shoulders helplessly as if to say: what on earth's that for? Then I picked up the whole caboodle and carried it over to the side of the stage as if to ask: please take it away, I don't need contraptions like that.

That turn always had them rocking in their seats. Jolly laughter rang out and even before I started singing I was rewarded with enthusiastic applause. By that time, half the battle was over. Thanks for the training, Viktor Viktorovich.

Then I gave a gracious nod to Asya and off we went.

The hall in that suburban metallurgical town was indeed first-class. It was spacious with a high ceiling and the walls were lined with lath that still seemed to smell of pine trees. The rows of seats were arranged in a semi-circle and the stalls sloped down steeply to the stage. It looked as if everyone from any part of the hall would have a good view of the stage, and be able to hear well.

As for the acoustics, Viktor Viktorovich had

not been exaggerating at all. I myself could hear how clearly my voice rang out, how every nuance of tone was caught. Not a single flexion was lost and even the softest of vibratos could be heard by all. Those same acoustics made the applause quite deafening when after "Santa Lucia" I gave them "Sole mio" and "Ritorna a Sorento". They just went wild.

On the quiet Asya dabbed her wet eyes as she turned over the pages. Viktor Viktorovich who was standing around in the wings grinned from ear to ear when I threw him a triumphant look from the stage. I did that at the moment when I realised once and for all that Maria Leontyevna had been wrong. She *was* a doctor, but as I had heard tell, doctors have been known to make mistakes. And this was going to be just such a case. She had made a mistake and it was as sure as houses that my voice had not yet started to break. Or perhaps—and that would be better still—it had already broken and all the worry was over. The thing was (that I had also heard tell) some people's voices broke instantaneously, overnight, and there you were with a new voice. Admittedly mine was still the old voice, which was a puzzle. Still there's no end to the miraculous things that happen in this life. At any rate there was no doubt about it though—in my case Maria Leontyevna was just plain wrong. I'd go on singing. I was singing for all I was worth.

I was giving them Schubert's "Ave Maria". Using my breath sparingly and at an even pace I started out on that long quiet "A-a-a . . ." at the beginning of the prayer. Everything was going fine and now I had to take the high notes.

But at the first high note I went skew-whiff. Suddenly my voice slipped out of key and made a desperate lurch like a billiard cue that only grazes the ball it's aiming for.

I managed to rescue the note and go on as if nothing had happened but Asya was so startled that she lost her place in the accompaniment for a moment. I felt my throat go tight, as if it was in an iron grip, and I strained and fought to escape that stranglehold. I shook it off but it had left its mark and a note of hoarseness appeared in my voice after that.

Oh, those damned acoustics! Now they were multiplying each tiny whisper of hoarseness or a scraped note five and ten times over and magnifying every lapse I made and every gasp for breath.

The hall was gripped in a deathly silence, like the one you get in a circus when a tightrope walker has got his eyes bound with a black cloth and gropes with his toes for the wire he cannot see and takes his first step, with no safety-net down below. . . .

I could feel how I was turning pale. I would have thought that the terrific strain on my vocal chords and the way I was tensing every muscle in my body ought to have made me turn purple. Yet all the same I could feel I was going ashen.

Yes, but all the same it was not for nothing that I had gone through Vladimir Konstantinovich Namestnikov's long tough training. That was the kind of training that would always see you through a crisis, and it saved me.

With my last ounce of strength I made my voice toe the line and got through to the end of that fatal "Ave Maria".

That was the end of my voice.

5

Afterwards I often thought to myself: and what if I hadn't ruined my voice at that concert? What if fate hadn't thrown me together with that wretched scoundrel? What if I hadn't made a habit of going to perform at those "pirate" concerts? If only I had listened to our dear old doctor Maria Leontyevna!

What would have happened then? Would I have kept my voice, or rather acquired a new one? Who knows? Perhaps I would. You never can tell. But now that the irretrievable had happened I was inclined to believe that I wouldn't have been able to go on singing anyway. It made me think back to my conversation with Kolya Biryukov during our visit to the Bird Market.

"We won't have any kind of voice."

"What! None at all?"

"Well, we'll still be able to talk of course, bla-bla-bla. . . ."

Yes, Kolya had been right. Bla-bla-bla—that was all that was left to me now. Incidentally, Kolya himself might well have had a pleasant surprise coming his way. He could set his hopes on a kinder fate, because he had not ruined his voice. He had just been told to give his voice a rest for the time being and he had kept quiet as he'd been told. As quiet as a mouse. Yet he'd made all those plans for his escape instead, which meant he hadn't had much faith in his turning out to be one of those lucky "one-in-a-thousand" boys.

What happens if someone had deep unshakable faith in his voice to come. Or if one took a firm grip on himself and for a time banished from his mind all that futile speculation as to whether he would have a voice or not? Perhaps in those cases Fate would be kinder and more merciful and reward a man's patience and faith.

I just wouldn't know. All I can say is, and this is jumping ahead a bit, that all the other chaps in our tuneful little class have had to forget they ever sang, except one lucky fellow. He started up again after his voice had broken and turned out to be that one in a thousand! But it wasn't me, alas. But who? I'll come to that secret all in good time.

That wisest of the wise, Nikolai Ivanovich Biryukov, had been right when he had said at the Bird Market that it was a law of Nature. And there's no getting round those, indeed that's precisely why they're called laws.

There was one other way of preserving your voice, although it's too dreadful to bear thinking about. Back in the old days, not just one hundred years ago, but several, and not here in Russia but at the Vatican, they used to subject boys to an infamous operation after which their voices never broke. Their voices could always soar heavenwards after that and always kept their angelic ring, they merely became more powerful with the years. Those voices were valued more than gold itself because every church in the land wanted to have its own angelic choir and, in particular, angel soloists. Some of those angels later became famous throughout the world. Their throats earned them fabulous riches, so much so that one of them, a certain Caffarelli, was able to permit himself the luxury of buying his own dukedom, thus making himself a duke. He sure did put on airs, that angel!. . . However there was no one for Caffarelli to leave his estates, his palace and his title to, for he was a duke without a duchess and one who could never hope for dukelets.

* * *

Now that so much water has flowed under the bridge since then, I am able to think back to what I went through after that disastrous concert without breaking into a cold sweat. But at the time I was quite frantic.

First of all I was summoned to the director's study; then there was a staff meeting about the incident and finally a Komsomol meeting. It all began when I had to have my throat examined the following Monday by Maria Leontyevna and she came out with her favourite phrase: "My little mirror tells me the whole story." Then one of the boarders went and split on me to Vladimir Konstantinovich (a really swinish thing to do, and no mistake) saying that I had acquired a suit of imported make, a nylon shirt and a cravat. It also emerged that some of the matrons had reported that Prokhorov had been missing on several occasions and only turned up late at night.

I didn't bother to deny it. Things could not be any worse than they were already. As it was, I was undescribably miserable.

I was sitting at a history of music lesson, holding my face in my hands and listening to what the teacher was telling us, or rather pretending to. I was feeling really cut up. The day before at the Komsomol meeting all the boys had voted that I should be severely cautioned and have an order mark recorded in my Komsomol file. They had all been there and supported the motion, Vitya Titarenko, Marat Aliev, and all the rest (except Georgi Vyazemsky who had skipped the meeting on purpose). It wasn't their unanimous decision that I was feeling cut up about. There was nothing much to be said on that score, after all I'd bent the rules, was definitely guilty and now was the time to repent—let them punish me, give me what I deserved with no holds barred. Although they could have skipped all the order mark business.

What riled me was that no one took into account that I had already received the harshest punishment of all, now that my voice was gone. I could always get my order mark erased on the strength of subsequent good conduct, earn a pardon so to speak. But my voice was something I could never get back. Never.... That was what really took the ground away from under my feet. I was well and truly floored this time, with no life in me, no voice left. Well and truly floored. Vitya Titarenko for one, what with him a Master of Sport and all, should have known that you don't hit a man when he's down. Yet he went ahead and.... Oh, what's the good....

I was listening absent-mindedly with only half an ear to what the teacher was telling us about Bach. I looked over to the wall. The lesson was in our classroom where there was a portrait of Johann Sebastian Bach on the wall. It showed him in an unfastened camisole with bronze buttons on the lapel and a waistcoat that wasn't buttoned up: he looked solid and dignified, with knitted brows and a stern expression on his face. His head was crowned with a bushy white wig. He was holding a sheet of music in one hand but you couldn't make out whether it was part of "The Brandenburg Concerto", "The Toccata in D Minor" or "The St. Matthew Passion"....

Great, inimitable Bach.

I'd played a lot of Bach in my time. When I had been very small I had played his charming

 "Piper's Tune" and the haunting "Menuetto". Those had been followed by the Inventions. The "Well-tempered Clavier" came next, then the Preludes and Fugues, pages and pages of them.

I used to spend many hours at the piano. Even in the days when I was still singing—when I was famous and made a fuss of by everyone and so happy—I didn't neglect the piano but remained loyal to the instrument that had first captured my imagination all those years ago in my orphanage days back in Lipetsk.

To be able to play the piano is essential for every musician, because it is the prince of instruments, their common denominator. At music schools and conservatoires violinists, flutists, drummers and singers, no matter what you specialise in, have to play the piano. There is no getting round it. Some people regard that compulsory discipline as a stupid drag. They don't like spending time on a subject which seems to them highly unnecessary. On their violins, for instance, they're about to catch up with David Oistrakh or at least Igor, while on the piano they're still bogged down in "Scenes from Childhood".

Incidentally I was once told that some jokester at the Gnesin Music Institute composed a special "Concerto for Compulsory Piano with Orchestra" in which the orchestra blares out the opening bars of Beethoven's Fifth while the pianist picks out a nursery rhyme with one finger.

But joking apart, for me the piano had always been something really sacred, something I'd taken really seriously. I had made a habit of playing a good deal and all those years Bach had been my constant companion and lodestar. I had been carried away more passionately by other composers from time to time, them I've already mentioned and will come back to later, but Bach was with me all the time nevertheless and will always be looking over my shoulder, so to speak.

Yes, Bach. I had read everything about him that I had been able to lay my hands on in the library and knew a good deal more than the required minimum for history of music exams. What was more I could relate an incident in which Johann Sebastian Bach himself was cautioned and given an order mark. There's no doubt about the order mark seeing that the document has been handed down to concerned posterity.

At the time he had been about seventeen, still very young. He had been working as church organist at Arnstadt where he used to have to play chorales before and after the sermon. The actual sermons sometimes used to last for a whole hour: once they got going, those preachers, there was no stopping them. But it was tedious for Bach just to sit there and twiddle his thumbs listening to those harangues. He used to slip down to the nearest tavern between chorales, the one before and the one after the sermon. There was plenty of time for a mug of beer and chat to his friends and then as the sermon was drawing to a close he would be back at his place ready to play the final chorale.

Then some low fellow reported him to the church dignitaries. Perhaps it was one of those very same "friends" who used to drink beer with him.

Then on another occasion young Johann Sebastian brought a girl to the church one night to play some of his early compositions to her. Where else could he have taken her for that purpose? At home he didn't even have a clavecin of his own, let alone an organ, so what could he have played on? It was perfectly natural to want to show off a little before a girl and what harm was there in it?

Yet once again someone reported him to the church dignitaries. Bach was summoned to appear before the church council to account for both misdemeanours, for running down to the tavern in the middle of the service and for bringing a "girl from outside" into the church at night. (Those were the very words used in the church records.) That very same "girl from outside" was his cousin Maria Barbara whom he was to marry soon afterwards. The poor soul died very young but the record of the incident has been handed down to this day.

Actually, the trouble he had from the dignitaries and his "friends" was a mere trifle. Bach's own children were to make fun of him at the end of his life, although he had made them what they were, respected members of society and accomplished musicians. They who owed everything to him laughed at their old father calling him "Old Wig" and boasting about their own talents as if they were a hundred times more gifted than he....

Great, inimitable Bach.

And hardly had he been laid to rest when the worthy citizens of his hometown decided to lay a road through the cemetery and dug over his grave, covering the place with cobble stones, so that to this day no one knows where lie the earthly remains of Johann Sebastian Bach.

I buried my face still deeper in my hands because I could feel tears welling up in my eyes.

I felt very sorry for Bach.

"Don't bother," said Georgi.
"Why?"
"Just don't. . . ."
"But why?"
"I tell you: don't bother."

That was news indeed. I was standing with Georgi Vyazemsky outside the Metro station. I had been asking him for a two-kopeck piece because I just had to make a telephone call and as luck would have it, I had no two-kopeck pieces on me, everything else under the sun, but none of the coins I needed. But Georgi wouldn't give me one; he just frowned, turned his face away and said: "Don't bother."

But the call was a matter of life and death, I just *had* to make it. A whole week had gone by since I had last seen Maya. At first I just hadn't been able to make it, what with the staff meeting and the session with the Komsomol. Then for several days at a stretch I had rung her at home but every time she had been out—at the library, or the theatre (without me too!), or some such place. Her mother informed me of her absence politely and with thorough explanations on each occasion. I had even started to wonder whether her Mamma on hearing about the trouble at the school had decided to protect her daughter from me. . . . In general, there was something I didn't really like about that Mamma. I put up with her purely because she was the mother of Maya and Georgi, Maya whom I was in love with and Georgi who was my friend.

Three days running I had been unable to get through to Maya. Every time it had been her mother who had answered the telephone, so today

I was planning to resort to cunning. I had decided to call Georgi to the rescue. Not only did he not seem to approve of my idea but he even insisted that he hadn't got any of those wretched two-kopeck pieces.

"You old miser!" I said angrily, handing him my big fifty-kopeck piece. "Take this."

This time it was his turn to lose his temper. He turned his pockets inside out, collected up all the silver and coppers in them, sifted through them and found a two-kopeck piece. Then he marched over to the row of telephone booths.

The two of us squeezed into one of the booths and Georgi dialled the number. "Mummy, that you? It's me. . . What? I'll be home soon. Is Maya home? Call her a minute, would you?"

Then he hurriedly pushed the receiver over to me.

"Hi!" came Maya's carefree voice down the line.

"Hallo," I said.

"What? Who's that?"

"It's me. Hallo," I repeated, smiling down the receiver.

At first there was no reply and then she answered in a quiet voice:

"Hallo."

Judging by her tone Maya was very frightened of her Mamma.

"Hallo," I said again. "When and where?"

Our telephone calls had always been brief and to the point: where and when. No unnecessary frills. Everything important we saved up till we met.

"I don't know," came her voice down the line still quieter and more cautious than before.

"Today," I went on, suggesting what I wanted most of all. "On Mayakovsky Square."

"I can't today. I've got a lot of homework. We've got a test tomorrow."

"Well, tomorrow," I said feeling a bit deflated. "Tomorrow at the same place."

"I can't tomorrow either," she went on with a sigh. "I've . . . I've got to go to the dressmaker's with Mummy."

"And the day after?" I said ever hopeful.

"The day after?" Maya's voice sounded more confident now than when she started out. "I can't possibly make it the day after, because that's Saturday and on Saturday I'm going to the Cinema Club. A girl-friend has got hold of tickets, just two, for her and me."

Yes, what a pity: only two. . . .

"Well, Sunday then," I said with a falter in my voice by that time because there would be a whole age to wait till Sunday.

"We've got visitors coming on Sunday," she informed me. "So, I can't make it then either."

"But when then?" I said completely at a loss by now, in the face of all those unfortunate engagements coming between the two of us. "When?"

"I don't know. . . ."

After those strange unexpected words the receiver seemed to go quite dead. All I could hear was the sound of breathing coming down it. Maya's breathing.

"Maya!" I called out desperately.

After that all that came out of the receiver was the engaged noise.

It was only when I was putting the receiver back that I noticed Georgi Vyazemsky was no longer in the booth. He was standing outside. When had he managed to slip out and why hadn't

I noticed and what had he disappeared for? Was it that he hadn't wanted to eavesdrop? Or simply that he couldn't bear to?

I stepped out of the booth. Georgi was looking at me with a disapproving frown and as if he was a bit sorry for me.

"Well, don't tell me I didn't warn you."

"What are you trying to say?"

"I told you not to bother."

Yes. He had said that. . . .

"So, it's your Mamma at the root of it all?" I asked, screwing up my eyes as I looked at him.

"A fat lot Mummy's got to do with it!" he hissed throwing me a threatening look. "She's got nothing to do with it. Don't you dare. . . . She's only guilty of one thing, telling you Maya wasn't home when in actual fact she was. It was Maya who made her lie to you. D'you get with it now? That's all there is to it. Now you know the whole story."

"But why?"

I asked him that question quite automatically, although the answer to it was something I could have got along very well without. One second had been enough to make me completely indifferent to the whole wide world.

Georgi hummed and hawed a bit and then said in a rather disgruntled voice:

"She's got a new craze. Some fellow's come along, a punny little weed, who plays chess." Then he went on in a more lively tone: "He's had a draw with Tigran Petrosyan though. It was at the Palace of Young Pioneers, where he took on forty players at once. Imagine it, a draw! At fifteen he managed to draw with Petrosyan. . . ."

"See you," I said and walked off.

"Zhenya . . ." he said running after me. "Zhenya, I'm going to a party this evening, where they've got a fantastic tape-recorder—a Grundig. Let's go along and get some dancing in, eh?"

I walked across the square in the opposite direction. I looked at the bare trees behind the Zoo railings that were glistening in the rain. The paths leading round the pond, that were usually so full of people, were quite empty now. The pond itself looked dead, a single pair of swans was gliding slowly round the little wooden house on the island and in the distance some ducks were shaking water off their feathers, looking all cold and miserable. The other birds had been shut up inside so that they wouldn't catch cold. Even those few remaining swans and quack-quacks should by all the laws have long since flown away to warmer climes. But of course they wouldn't be flying away anywhere: they were used to wintering in the Zoo or, if my information was reliable, their wings had been clipped to make quite sure that they would stay behind.

Yet, as had always been the case in autumn, there had been a marked increase in another group of the Zoo's inmates that did not merit any special identification plaques but who came of their own free will to live at the Zoo: the branches of the bare trees were black with the squawking crows and down on the muddy paths below there were busy little groups of sparrows to be seen.

Yes, winter was just round the corner. Another winter.

By the entrance to the Zoo, a woman in a white overall on top of her coat was selling ice-cream. She was always standing there, come wind, come rain, selling ice-cream.

But during all those years I'd never really paid any attention to her. I'd walked past her several times a day but never taken a closer look at her. Somehow she'd eluded my gaze, probably because I wasn't allowed to notice her, neither her, nor her stall. The stern ban imposed at that very spot by the entrance so long ago, had been in force ever since.

It was only now as I walked up to the gates leading into the Zoo that I saw or rather discovered that it was not just a woman in a white overall selling ice-cream, but the ice-cream seller who had been standing there so long ago, a hundred years before. I recognised her, it was the same elderly woman. What was so amazing was that for the last hundred years that very same ice-cream seller had not changed in the slightest and was exactly the same as I remembered her, whereas I had changed so much in those eight years that she of course couldn't possibly recognise me.

No, of course she wouldn't have recognised me. To be honest I found it hard to recognise myself, not only the Zhenya I had been on that distant day when I had first arrived in Moscow but also the boy I had been a week before, two days before, a mere hour before.

I walked up to the ice-cream seller, held out my fifty-kopeck piece and said:

"One eskimo-pie, please."

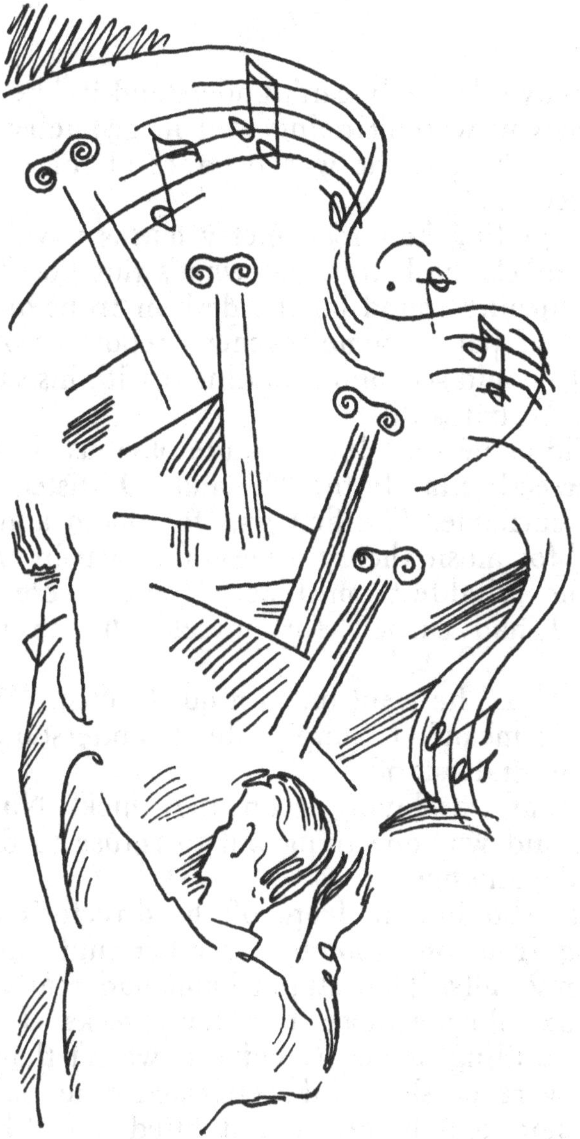

PART FOUR

"Zhenya, I simply can't understand it," he said. "When you weren't doing well in geometry that was one thing ... it was disgraceful, of course, however. . . ."

"I'm getting better geometry marks now."

"So much the better, but what's this here?" he asked turning round on the desk in front of him a sheet of paper, some teacher's report or other, so that I could see, and prodding it with his sallow finger. "What *is* this?"

Couldn't he see? It was quite obvious. I could see perfectly plainly the "C" and "D" listed next to my surname. The first was for piano and the second for music theory. Everything was in order, not the slightest mistake. Those were the marks I had earned for myself the previous week.

"Zhenya," he went on in a quiet voice. "What does this mean? I simply don't understand. I refuse to understand!"

But that was laying it on too thick. Not to understand was one thing but to refuse to do so was quite another.

I was standing in front of the director's desk shifting from one foot to the other and pulling down my cuffs. That stupid habit had really got its claws into me those last few weeks. I was forever pulling down my cuffs. It wasn't that my sleeves were too short; I'd been issued a new school jacket not long before and it fitted me like a glove. Yet I was shooting up at a fantastic rate all the time. Sometimes it was even as if I could feel myself growing, feel my neck and my head on top of it gradually pushing upwards, feel my toes getting cramped in my shoes and my hands pushing out of my sleeves, that I kept pulling down.

"I'll do something about it." Of course I would, there were no two ways about it. Otherwise I'd find myself with no grant money for the next six months.

"Zhenya, sit down, please," said Vladimir Konstantinovich, pushing the report over to one side. "You must explain to me now. . . ."

What was there to explain?

"I'll do something about it," I repeated in a hollow voice.

I couldn't bring myself to explain to him that I hated music theory and my piano lessons into the bargain, that I hated all music.

* * *

Well, perhaps that was going a bit too far or even quite up the creek—I didn't feel any real hate, of course. It was just that I couldn't care less about it any more. I didn't go to singing practice any more, there were no concerts any more. For the first time in my life I felt that horrible feeling of being at a loose end, and it made me lose my bearings. Homework? Well, that was something one could either take seriously or turn one's back on. Piano lessons? Well, that was up to you too: either sit down and practice or turn your back on it and up and away.

I just upped and away. . . .

When you up and away in Moscow there are plenty of interesting things to go and do, even if it's just wandering up and down Presnya getting to know every corner of it.

I liked wandering past the quiet old houses on

Bolshaya Gruzinskaya and Malaya Gruzinskaya streets, peering up at their façades that were like people's faces, each with an individual character of their own. Those inscrutable stone faces undoubtedly guarded some fascinating secrets. For some time by then I had been quite sure that all those old houses were brimming over with secrets, our school building among them.

Once, when I was still in Form VIII, some people turned up at our school armed with files and plans and then they were followed by some others bringing hammers and iron crow-bars. Referring to their plans as they went, they started knocking away at the walls first on the ground floor, then the first floor and finally in the cellar. They kept on knocking away and listening. Later, during break, we noticed that they had started breaking up part of the wall.

We, of course, found it practically impossible to sit through our lessons. The knocking noise was the only thing we were paying attention to and everyone was hazarding guesses as to what it was all about. Some people said that they were looking for a hidden treasure, while others maintained that they were searching for a bomb that had fallen into the building during the war, but had not exploded and was still stuck in the school wall somewhere. It made you feel rather jumpy, still it was fun to watch all the goings-on.

But things didn't progress any further after that. They didn't appear to have found anything. Instead they just patched up the wall again, collected up their plans and tools and went off again apologising for the inconvenience.

Yet it turned out that they really had been searching for a treasure. I discovered the fact from a reliable source, from Polina Romanovna, our concierge, whom I described earlier. She, after all, had been sitting by our school door underneath the silent brass bell since time immemorial. She actually lived in a dilapidated little wooden house out in the back yard that the demolition squads never seemed to get round to, probably because you couldn't see it from the street.

It goes without saying that Polina Romanovna knew all there was to know about the mansion which now housed our school.

One winter evening I had been sitting late at the piano (in those days I used still to spend quite a lot of time at the piano) and on my way down the stairs I stopped for a little chat with Polina Romanovna, asking whether there were perhaps any more unexpected letters for me, how she was feeling and what she thought of the weather. And that was not very long after the men had been round to knock at the wall and take part of it to pieces.

Polina Romanovna was obviously glad to have someone to talk to on that long winter evening, and to pass the time she told me the following story.

In the past the building that now housed our school had been the home of a rich Moscow merchant, a Councillor of State by the name of Pyotr Ivanovich Shchukin, the owner of several mills in and around Moscow. Originally though he had lived in another building not on Bolshaya Gruzinskaya Street, but Malaya Gruzinskaya Street, quite near at hand. There he had resided in a magnificent palace specially built for him: he had stipulated that it should resemble an ancient boyar's terem complete with ornamental pillars, eaves and porches, the only difference being that it was all to be of stone and brick, instead of wood, and what's more, faced with tiles. The palace stands in Malaya Gruzinskaya Street to this day. I've been there and looked at it, it's a rather impressive building.

But that palace made no really appreciable dent in Pyotr Shchukin's fortune; he still had more money than he could use and his capital, instead of shrinking, continued to grow. It was then that he decided to start collecting. But he didn't collect stamps, matchbox labels or sweet-wrappers as people do nowadays, his passion was something quite different. He started to collect Russian antiques, gold vases, silver platters, crystal goblets and fine porcelain. He also went in for ancient manuscripts, swords and sabres and brocade finery. In other words, he collected everything he could lay his hands on that was of historic interest.

This passion for collecting works of art and historic treasures was quite common among rich Moscow merchants: their collections grew apace, they set up whole galleries and they brought home to Russia countless wonders from all corners of the globe.

Pyotr Ivanovich's younger brothers also went in for the same kind of thing. Dmitri travelled round Europe and bought up pictures by ancient masters while Sergei preferred contemporary works: he came home from Paris bringing with him dazzling canvases by Monet, Degas and Renoir.

By that time their elder brother had such a fabulous collection of art treasures in his palace on Malaya Gruzinskaya Street that it was now more like a museum than a home. Indeed, one day Pyotr Shchukin decided that if it was so like a museum, a museum it should become. With that he presented it to the Historical Museum, to the

City of Moscow, complete with all its priceless contents.

For himself he bought a smaller residence on Bolshaya Gruzinskaya Street, the one that is now our school, and died soon after he had settled in there. But before he died he had bricked up his private fortune.

He must have bricked it up. After all when demolition work got going to make way for New Arbat, the most impressive of the city's new avenues, in virtually every one of the houses that had been inhabited by wealthy merchants before the revolution the excavators had only to take one knock at the walls before gold coins, necklaces and heaven knows what else started tumbling out. I'd read about it all in the newspapers, in the Moscow evening paper.

This was enough to convince every boy at the school that there were riches bricked up in the walls of the school. After the official investigators with their plans and picks had been and gone, we boys spent a whole year rummaging around on our own account. It became something of a habit with all of us: we used to walk down the corridors knocking against the walls with our knuckles, at various levels, ears pricked for any unusual sound. However, those enormously thick walls of the old building only responded to our efforts with one and the same dead thud wherever we tried.

Where was the treasure trove? It must have been somewhere, the wretched thing!

Only Polina Romanovna used to shake her head and say that Pyotr Shchukin's riches were all in the Historical Museum and the collections belonging to Sergei and Dmitri in Volkhonka Street.

* * *

I had been to Volkhonka Street, or rather the Fine Arts Museum, before. The whole school had been taken round it to be initiated in yet another aspect of our cultural heritage.

But that first visit had left me with a rather unpleasant impression. I mustn't leave that incident out if I'm going to be honest to the end. You see, among the pictures that hung in that gallery were a great many showing naked women. Some of them had a minimum of covering and others were completely uncovered. There were also statues on the same theme.

I personally wasn't bothered by that in the slightest. I knew quite well that painters and sculptors loved to extol the beauty of the human form in their work and so I didn't see anything "shameful" in it: I just walked round the gallery and looked at all the exhibits.

But there's no getting away from it, schoolboys do behave rather foolishly in places where such works of art are on display. The thing was that apart from us there were other school kids there that day from ordinary secondary schools. While the girls behaved quite normally and contemplated the great works with serious, awe-inspired interest on their faces and jotted things down in their little note-books, some of the boys were making real fools of themselves, nudging each other, winking and giggling every time they came across a painting or statue depicting a nude. Actually, I think that it was a sign of embarrassement rather than irreparable depravity. But when people behave like that all around you, you can't help feeling awkward too and even getting angry at yourself.

But now I used to go to that gallery on my own. Now that I was at a loose end, I was making the most of my unwelcome leisure.

So I wandered around the town and I often went to the Fine Arts Museum. At that particular moment when I had lost all interest in music—or at any rate music theory—for some reason or other I developed a real passion for that museum, where there was no trace of any music, but where at every visit I experienced the same joy that music had always brought me in the past. There was something very radiant about that joy. Radiant in the literal sense of the word, pouring forth light.

Sometimes out in the country you can be walking along with green woods to one side of you and a blue stream on the other, along a narrow path winding through corn that sways in the wind and is dotted with cornflowers and daisies. Everything all round you is beautiful, a real sight for sore eyes, but the sun is missing, hidden behind a cloud and everything is under a fine veil of shadow. Then suddenly—quite unexpectedly, like a flash of lightning—the sun peeps out from behind the clouds and everything before you is transformed.

The wood is still green, the stream blue and the daisies white, yet how everything has changed! The green is quite different, so are the white and the blue. Everything has changed in this new, dazzling, incredibly sunlit world!

That's what happened to me in the gallery on Volkhonka Street.

I walked round at a leisurely pace, following the curve of the walls as I passed from one hall into another. There were pictures at every step: woods and fields, rivers and mountains, faces, tables laden with game and fruit, streets and squares in unfamiliar cities. Here and there you could see cavalry and infantry locked in combat, here and there declarations of love were being uttered. Yet all these pictures without exception were overcast: the mountains, the streets, the skirmishes were going on in the shade and the lovers were kissing in the shade. Actually, in some of the pictures you could pick out places that were lit up by the sun, next to the places in shadow. Yet—how should I explain it—the sunlit places still seemed overcast somehow, they were just a little brighter than those completely immersed in shade.

Then suddenly when I crossed the threshold of a new hall, everything changed. It was as if the sun which had been hidden by clouds for a long time suddenly broke out from behind them. I was dazzled and involuntarily screwed up my eyes. I even wondered for a moment if I had taken the wrong door without noticing it and instead of coming into another hall of the museum had come straight out of the quiet twilight into the bright summer street outside.

Yet I opened my eyes again and saw that I was still in the museum after all. The pictures on the wall in that hall depicted similar things to those I had seen in all the others, the same eternal themes to which so many artists have turned—woods and mountains, bridges and churches, faces, bodies and flowers.

But what all-pervading light flooded them! What scorching brightness there was in those patches of sun, how fresh and cool the shade looked. The air streamed, flowed and rippled and was heady with the scent of flowers. The leaves on the trees rustled palpably, and the sea was crashing down on the rocks. The women's eyes were liquid and gentle. Such clean colours, such pulsing life.

After that revelation I spent hours on end looking at those pictures trying to fathom how the amazing effect had been achieved. I studied them in detail and after closer scrutiny I was able to pick out the characteristic features of the brush strokes—Monet's generous sweeps, rows of tiny dabs of colour in Van Gogh's work, and Renoir's colours that flowed one out of the other.

* * *

I walked out of the museum and past the colonnade at the front entrance, stopped for a moment on the broad flight of steps leading down to the lawn outside and sat down on one of them.

It was a hot sunny day and people were taking hasty steps as if the asphalt was scorching their heels. Their clothes were colourful and summery, a kaleidoscope of cotton dresses and casual shirts. Youth predominated, and understandably so, seeing the University was a stone's throw away, not to mention the Lenin Library and the city's largest swimming pool. Part of the street was roped off and behind a fence painted red and white women from a road-maintenance team were touching up white lines on the black asphalt. The cars were having to go round them in single file, green, blue, yellow, grey and even pink cars, and the traffic lights were flashing red, amber and green to add still more colours to the scene.

Everything round about was bright, noisy and had a festive air. I sat there on the steps of the museum feeling lonely and miserable. I had lost my voice. I had lost Maya. Back there in the gallery behind me were exhilarating pictures pulsing with life, although their creators had long since left this earth. Wonderful day-to-day life was seething and throbbing on the thoroughfare before me.

But I felt divorced from it all somewhat, as I sat on the steps: I had lost my bearings, and had lost all that was most important to me. The feeling reminded me of the far-off day when I had got lost in the Zoo. I had been a real tiddler then, on my first day in Moscow. That very first day I had got lost, sat down on the nearest bench and started crying. But had I actually cried on that occasion? No, of course I hadn't. I'd got up, looked around me and gone on my way. And that had been the right thing to do.

I got up and went on my way. The asphalt really was so hot that it scorched the soles of your feet even through shoe-leather. I quickened my pace and on this occasion no one overtook me, I just walked on with the crowd, caught up in their energetic impetuous surge forward, so typical of Muscovite pedestrians on week-days during working hours.

The human tide carried me with it to Manezhnaya Square, Gorky Street and Red Square.

It was then all of a sudden that I caught that sound, that is, I became conscious of the noise of steps, my steps and the steps of all the people around me. But they were more than ordinary footfalls now, they were steps in the bass register: "trrum-tum-tum-tum . . . trrum-tum-tum-tum. . . ." First high, then low, then high again. Those bass phrases repeated themselves in the same pattern and rhythm. Obstinate basses, in fact the musical term for them reflects that—basso ostinato—stubborn would be a better adjective for them! "Trrum-tum-tum-tum. . . ."

I noticed that the little finger and thumb of my left hand had started of their own accord to stretch a whole octave and were moving up and down in time with the rhythm I could hear. So much for my left hand, but what about the right?

I listened hard but for the time being I couldn't pick out the actual melody. I could only sense vaguely what my right hand should do. It must of course clash slightly with the obstinate chords in the bass—it was as if my right hand was going to show them that it would disrupt their precise pattern, however tenacious they might be, and break up the rhythm. Here you are for a start: "ta-ta, ta-ta, ta-ta . . ." harsh, stark syncopation. Or still better a patch of Morse, using all five fingers of my right hand in turn, to rattle out a staccato on one and the same high key, lingering for a second on the dashes.

Then to blend it all in together. . . .

There was a wild scream of brakes and a militia-man's whistle rent the air. A bus ground to a halt right in front of my very nose. Heavens! I'd forgotten that you're not allowed to cross there and that they'd only recently made an underpass at that very spot. Looking round furtively at the militia-man I rushed over to the underpass with the bus-driver hurling abuse after me.

I ran through the tunnel, but strangely enough I didn't feel a bit frightened, rather exhilarated in fact. It was because I knew, because I was quite convinced, that even if that stupid bus had knocked me over and I had found myself flat out on the ground and unable to get up, but still alive of course, and people had come running up from all directions and the whine of an ambulance siren had started up in the distance while I lay there face downwards and unconscious—even then the fingers of my left hand would have gone on beating out that persistent rhythm down in the bass octaves while the fingers of my right hand would have gone on pecking away at one and the same spot, rattling out Morse signals.

2

To be honest, it had all started before that. It was just that I hadn't taken it seriously before.

It had been back in the old days when I had still had a voice. It was in the summer when we were out in the Young Pioneer camp at Vereya and I was missing Maya very badly: in an effort to take my mind off her I used to play the piano a great deal. I used to spend whole days by myself on the verandah where there was an old Becker upright. Meanwhile the others would be swimming in the nearby river and sunbathing, catching butterflies or just fooling about, in other words, getting on with what normal children are expected to be doing when they are on holiday.

And there was I always at the piano. . . . In those days my two idols were Chopin and Scriabin, or rather I was deserting one of these two idols for the other, Chopin for Scriabin. Scriabin himself did a great deal to promote that change in my priorities. While playing his compositions I came to feel quite tangibly how Alexander Nikolayevich Scriabin had also come to grips with Chopin's all-powerful influence and then reached out beyond it. Indeed Scriabin's early pieces owe a good deal to Chopin, and as I see it not in the least because he imitated the great Pole or borrowed from his writing. Not in the slightest! It was just that they were very similar as people in their sensitivity and the turbulent restlessness of their spirit.

Scriabin was soon however to break out on his own and find his own style and he took me along with him.

I worked away at Scriabin's Third Sonata till my fingers were at breaking-points . . . but I couldn't master it. I just didn't seem to have enough fingers. Perhaps my hands were too small? But how could *he* have coped with it? I knew that he had had small hands, almost like a child's. So he, too, must have had a tough struggle, straining his wrists to the utmost to cope with those monstrous chords, that he himself had conjured up, those incredible passages.

Once he played so hard that his right hand was paralysed and it was then that he wrote his "Prelude for the Left Hand".

No, thanks, I didn't fancy going to any such extremes. I lifted my hands from the keyboard, gave them a good shake and straightened my tired shoulders. That would do for one day.

Yet my hands, almost of their own accord, started reaching out for the black and white keys all over again. Just how on earth had Scriabin coped with those chords?

To start with I took an E octave starting at E above middle C. That was easy. But the chord sounded empty, naked somehow. So now to take the bottom E down a tone and there I was! There it was—a ninth, a nona, an attractive word, that could have been a girl's name. It was a nice word, but the interval itself wasn't too kind on the ear. I'm not wary of dissonance, but. . . . Here was where the trick came. If I filled out that nona with three other notes, spaced out evenly in between, then a miracle took place. The harsh unpleasant dissonance suddenly ripples forth in a sparkling harmony, a delight to the ear—a nonachord.

Scriabin loved to use those nonachords and I like them too. But at that particular moment I was faced with a different task—training my hands. Training—that was everything. Now I had to raise the top-note of the chord by a semitone—up you go, you blasted little finger, u-up. . . . Had I made it? Yes. So what did that give me? A tenth, a decima. Splendid.

Now to go back to the beginning and go through all that again. First the two E's, then down for the D and up to the F. . . . Stop, stop! If I made the bottom E a fraction short and carried over the second one, that of itself would set a rhythm going, probably $^3/_4$ time. As for the F at the top of the chord, that now demanded some natural resolution of the whole weird melody.

Melody? Yes—melody. Where had it sprung from? I didn't know. I'd just been playing a series of large intervals, an eighth, a ninth and then a tenth. Now I had my $^3/_4$ time, and a waltz rhythm, and A minor. And now what if I should follow that up with a broken chord over a ninth in another key down in the bass, by way of accompaniment, "one, two, three"?

* * *

Is that really how music is written? And indeed was that really music?

I don't know. How could I insist that it was? For who can explain how music is written, how it comes into being? Especially if it takes shape under your very own fingers.

Yet I have tried to put all that into words honestly, just as it happened. That was how it happened with me.

When it was nearly time for lunch Georgi Vyazemsky popped up like a Jack-in-the-box: he was as brown as a berry and wearing nothing but a pair of shorts and a garland of rosehips round his neck. He vaulted on to the verandah and perched on the balustrade that ran round it. By then I was no longer just groping for notes but playing my "Nona-waltz" fairly confidently. ("Nona-waltz" was the name it had acquired by then.)

Georgi listened for a bit, then swung his other leg over the balustrade, walked over and inquired casually: "Is that Prokofiev?"

A real connoisseur he was!

"Yeah," I replied.

He listened for a bit more and then acknowledged condescendingly, "Not bad nonachords."

"Yeah," I agreed.

He listened for a bit more and then said: "And you know, Zhenya: all that can be worked out mathematically."

"What d'you mean 'worked out'?" I said in surprise, interrupting my playing.

"Yes, all of it. Worked out mathematically.... Now if you take an octave, for instance, you've got a ratio of two to one—when it comes to the frequency of vibrations. It's a straightforward ratio. But if you take a ninth, then you're up against something much more complicated, but you can still work it out mathematically and a nonachord's much simpler. You can do it with anything in music!"

"But what for?" I asked.

"Wait a moment," Georgi went on, getting really carried away by this time. "Now how many sounds are there in one of your octaves on the piano here?"

"Twelve. . . ."

There was no end to my surprise. Surely Georgi Vyazemsky hadn't managed to forget everything he'd spent so many years learning in the course of a single summer? Or had he just spent too much time out in the sun that day? He was fantastically brown. . . .

"Twe-elve!" Georgi exclaimed with a mocking laugh. "Not twelve but eighty-five. The Ancients knew that, Pythagoras himself worked it out. Have you cottoned on? But there are just twelve on the keyboard so as to make life simpler. . . . Just imagine having to cope with all eighty-five of them!"

"But what for?" I asked.

"What d'you mean 'what for'?"

"What I say—twelve are quite enough for me."

"But not for me," persisted Georgi and started angrily twiddling the heathen beads hanging round his neck. "In fact eighty-five probably wouldn't be enough for me. . . ."

"Why?" I said casting a concerned glance in his direction. Georgi Vyazemsky didn't look on top form that day. He wasn't sickening for something, was he?

Suddenly, despite his scant attire, Georgi struck a commanding pose and announced in solemn tones:

"I have verified harmony with algebra!" Then

he wiped his forehead, thought for a moment and rephrased his pronouncement: "No, not quite that. . . . 'With algebra I have verified harmony.' With it?"

"What?" I said, at a loss to follow what he was on about.

"Tut, tut! That's Pushkin, from *Mozart and Salieri*. Have you read it?"

"Well and so what?" I asked. To be quite honest though, I had not read the piece. It had not been on our syllabus and somehow I just hadn't got round to it in my free time. Nevertheless I still had some idea what it was all about. I knew that Salieri poisoned his best friend Mozart in it. Sometimes you come across friends like that.

"Well and so what?" I asked again, just to be on the safe side.

"Well, just this," Georgi replied harshly. "I've gone and got carried away with algebra, old chap. Algebra pure and simple, with no more harmony or music thrown in. I'm going to try for a place at the University physics faculty."

"Go on with you," I said, unable to believe my ears.

"It's all decided, Zhenya. The only trouble is there's very fierce competition to get in." He sighed and added: "I'll have to start doing extra classes at evening school in the autumn."

3

That autumn a good number of boys in our class enrolled for classes at evening school. We were lucky it was so near, not just near but in the very same building as our hostel, only the entrance was from the other side. Yet it was no light burden that the boys were taking on: imagine studying in two places at once and doing two lots of homework.

Georgi Vyazemsky and Vitya both enrolled at evening school and several others from our fraternity of the voiceless. I was not one of them though.

Some people may wonder why on earth should boys who were already studying at one school start doing courses at another? What lay behind that superhuman hunger for learning?

It was quite simple to explain really, although the situation itself was far from simple. The thing was that when we completed our ten years at the music school we would not be given any school leaving certificate. Ours was no ordinary school, not even a school with a special bias, but a choir school, that turned out qualified musicians. Instead of an ordinary school leaving certificate we would be given a document complete with a stamp bearing a coat of arms to show that we had spent ten years at the music school and had qualified as full-fledged musicians. It showed that we had already had a specialised training and were entitled to teach others. That document enabled us to start work right away, at a school for instance, as a singing master.

Unfortunately singing is not something that is taken seriously at school, it's looked upon as something that is no use to anyone in this modern age of ours.

Take the story of Vladik Tsifrin for instance. He left our school the year before last and was then taken on as a singing master in one of Moscow's schools. It should be noted in passing that Vladik didn't cut what you'd call an impressive figure, being short and puny with even a rather sickly look about him.

Well, so he turned up to take his first lesson. It was fifth-formers he found himself up against. He had a madhouse on his hands right from the start. Those fifth-formers were strapping lads, real loutish bullies, all a good head taller than he was. At the mere sight of him they clutched their stomachs in helpless laughter and the girls, foolish creatures, started giggling away and, worse still, kept egging the boys on. After waiting for a bit Vladik sat down at the piano and said: "Children, choral art came into being in the distant past—" At those words the class collapsed completely and started crawling around on all fours, miaowing, barking and getting up to Heaven knows what. Then Vladik Tsifrin tried again, in a sterner tone this time: "Stop this disgraceful behaviour, remember you're at school not at home." But that didn't help either. One of the louts turned on a pocket transistor full blast, and, with his mouth wide open, started doing an Elvis Presley turn, while two other pupils let fly with a rock-and-roll number there and then in the middle of the lesson. Then Vladik got up and said in a quiet voice: "I'm warning you, I only hit out twice: once across the head and the next time down on the coffin-lid." (And that was weedy little Vladik threatening beefy great fifth-formers.) What else was there for him to do? The important thing was that it worked like magic: all the bullies took fright, went quiet and took up their places round the piano and Vladik managed to proceed with his first lesson with no further mishap.

However those holy horrors went straight to their parents to complain about the teacher who had threatened to attack them, and all the indignant Mammas and Papas came running to the headmaster. The upshot of it all was that Vladik Tsifrin had to leave the school the next day. He is now in charge of the choral society at a biscuit factory.

In addition to those enticing prospects, the certificate you are given on leaving the choir school entitles you to go on studying music, to enrol at the Conservatoire or the Gnesin Music Institute for instance. There people are only too happy to take on our boys because they know the kind of grounding Vladimir Konstantinovich's protégés have had. If you count up all the conductors and choir-masters who started out on their musical careers at our school it's enough to make you gasp, there are so many famous names.

So when all's said and done the leaving certificate they gave us at the choir school was a piece of paper worth having. It was a useful document and guaranteed us our daily bread.

* * *

All the same a lot of the boys started going to evening classes that autumn. They needed an ordinary school certificate and that was all there was to it.

After all, then we'd first been brought along to the school, little whipper-snappers of seven or eight, not one of us had started giving much serious thought to the question of what he wanted to be when he grew up. Now all of a sudden it turned out that by no means all the boys felt the urge to be choir-masters, not everyone was champing at the bit to teach singing to unmanageable adolescents or was attracted by the prospect of spending his working life in a biscuit factory.

It was at that very time that Vitya Titarenko suddenly announced that he wanted to join the army.

"Be a conductor in the army?" I asked him.

"No, I just want to join up," said Vitya laughing for no apparent reason. "I want to go to the Military Academy."

"Oh-ho, so that's it! Another budding cosmonaut, I presume."

"No," said Vitya Titarenko shaking his head, "I want to be an officer in the infantry."

"But why?" I asked in surprise.

"What d'you mean 'why'?" Vitya asked, sounding quite irritated by this time. "I want to be in the army, to be an officer. Surely you understand?"

"Oh, so that's how it is," I said, catching on at last. "Well, that makes everything quite clear. That must be because the Central Army Sports Club lured you away from the Burevestnik Club. That right?"

"Rot," said Vitya looking at me with undisguised contempt. "No one lured me away, on the contrary I went round to try and join the CASC quite off my own bat. Perhaps that'll make some difference when my application is considered. D'you realise what a lot of people try to get into the Military Academy?" Vitya paused to think for a moment and then went on: "And what's more you have to have an ordinary school certificate. Our school papers aren't enough, for the most important things for the Military Academy are maths and physics, while here we hardly touch them."

"And what about music?" I asked.

In answer to that question Vitya merely shrugged his shoulders in a vague fashion.

I put the same blunt question to Georgi Vyazemsky when he started going to evening classes and swatting away for the entrance exams to the physics and mathematics faculty. He had set himself the goal of not merely getting his ordinary school certificate but getting a distinction as well.

"You see, nobody who hasn't got a distinction ever tries for it," he explained, "There is enough competition among those who have got distinctions as it is, can you imagine it?"

"And what about music?" I asked.

"Music?" Georgi echoed with an elusive smile. "There'll be plenty of time for that. If I get in I'll lose no time in rustling up a little jazz group. How about 'Swinging Tangents' for a name, perhaps? And we'll walk off with all the prizes at all amateur contests! That's something that the University authorities always appreciate. You know there's a chap at our evening classes who's also planning to try and get into the physics and maths faculty—now he would be just the person to round up for something like that: you see he writes songs himself. By the way, Zhenya, I'd like you to meet him. We're having a get-together tomorrow, everyone from the evening classes I go to—they're a nice bunch and some of the girls are good fun too. . . . Are you coming?"

"I don't know."

"What's knowing got to do with it? We'll just pop along—and that's all there is to it."

Was Georgi tenacious the way he used to insist I went along to all those parties of his! Heaven knows why.

"Well, are you coming?"

"All right, I'll come," I finally agreed.

And the next evening Georgi and I really did go along to one of those parties of his. I'll come to that party later, but I mustn't forget something more important, far more important.

* * *

Marat Aliev—he was the person who was to be the one in a thousand blessed by Fate.

His voice started to break earlier than anyone else's in our class and he rested it longer than all the others, for a whole two years. When at last he opened his mouth again his voice turned out to be a baritone and what a baritone! Its timbre was like that of Lisitsian's voice and I would say richer still—may Pavel Lisitsian forgive me, and indeed perhaps we were mistaken, for after all Marat Aliev was a boy from our class, from our hostel.

We were so impressed by Marat's voice that almost every evening before we went to sleep we used to force him to sing, bring physical pressure to bear. He'd try and shake us off, saying, "I want to sleep." But we would demand that he start singing that instant, or else.... Then poor old Marat would give a deep sigh, stand right up on his bed, wrapped in his sheets, fold his hands across his stomach, raise his chin and start up with:

To thee, God of nuptias, I sing,
To thee who dost join
The bride and groom...

We held our breath as we listened such was the power of that voice, and voices were something we were well up in. After all we too had had decent voices once upon a time.

Praise and Glory
To Croesa and Nero,
Praise and Glory...

By now you would be able to hear bare feet pattering about in the corridor, for boys from the next-door dormitory would be creeping up to the door to listen; sooner or later the whole hostel would be there to listen to the "concert", to listen to Marat Aliev.

Meanwhile Marat himself would have got carried away, and forgotten that he had wanted to go to sleep. His enormous eyes would look inspired and stern. Rubinstein's "Epitalama" might be followed by Eugene Onegin's confessions of love, the "Song of the Guest from Vedenegi" or *Figaro, Figaro, Fi-i-igaro....*

Eventually though we ourselves would be finding it difficult to keep our eyes open and start having the odd surreptitious yawn as we struggled to keep awake. But Marat standing up there on his bed would just sing on and on.

The last summer holidays before he was due to leave school he spent in his hometown and a few days after the new term began a sleek black Chaika drew up at the school porch. It was during break-time, so we were all able to see and hear everything that took place.

Two black figures got out of the black Chaika, men with black hair, thick black eyebrows and big black eyes just like Marat's. They were dressed in austere black suits, black ties and black ankle-boots. Their lapels bristled with all kinds of important insignia that looked like lots of different coloured flags.

Later we were to discover that they were the Minister of Culture and the Permanent Representative in Moscow of the Caucasian republic that was Marat Aliev's home.

The important visitors went up the stairs and then disappeared behind the tall white door leading into the director's study. As soon as they were inside we clustered round the door and started listening for all we were worth. We were very curious to know what was going on, and incidentally eavesdropping outside the study on that occasion was fool's play because once the opening niceties had been exchanged the conversation proceeded fortissimo.

"No, on no account. The boy must finish his schooling here...."

"Don't worry, Comrade Director, he will complete it at another music school."

"He will go on to study at the Moscow State Conservatoire!"

"We have our own conservatoire, also a state one, every bit as good."

"But it's here that he's been trained! We made a man and a musician of him...."

"Comrade Director, he was born in our republic and it is we who shall make a musician of him."

"I'm going to ring Yekaterina Alexeyevna up here and now!" threatened Vladimir Konstantinovich, so worked up by that time that he was quite out of breath.

"But we have already been to see the Minister of Culture about him. She asked us to convey her warm regards to you..." replied the visitors in a conciliatory tone.

To cut a long story short, they kidnapped Marat, carried him off. That same black Chaika swept him away from the school to Vnukòvo Airport.

The next spring he won the first prize at an international singing competition.

* * *

Not long afterwards I finally met those friends of Georgi Vyazemsky's at one of his countless parties.

They were a rather jolly, friendly crowd, all lads from his evening classes and all passionate mathematicians. Among others, I met the boy whom Georgi had told me about, the one whom he hoped to rope into his "Swinging Tangents" band. He was a great character and really did compose songs. In fact, we spent the whole evening just listening to the songs he had composed. They weren't at all bad. One of them was about a tram who was bored of crawling up and down along its rails and one day drove right off them to run away into the woods where he could frisk about on the green grass to his heart's content. Another was about a football that everyone was kicking cruelly and only the goalkeeper clasped tenderly to his bosom, despite all its mud and scratches. Then there was another. . . .

But the most important thing was that the fellow made up everything himself: the words, the music and what was more it was he who sang all those songs accompanying himself on the guitar most competently. At one stage I asked him:

"Where did you learn to play?"

"Nowhere," he answered. "I taught myself."

"What about composing?"

"I taught myself that too."

"And song-writing?"

"That too, and how to sing."

Some people just don't know how lucky they are! They just have it made, it all comes naturally. It's little more than a joke or a game to them and yet they don't make a bad job of things at all.

With other dull sloggers though . . . but that's enough of that.

At that party I also met a girl with red hair done up in a pony-tail. Georgi introduced her to me and sat us next to each other at table. After the party I saw her home to the Noviye Kuzminki district and in the porchway we spent a whole hour snogging. She made a date for the next day but I didn't turn up. Why, I wonder? Anyone's guess, perhaps I should have gone. She was a perfectly nice girl.

4

"Zhenya, Zhenya!"

Once again there was Usachov, my namesake, shaking me by the shoulder: the little pest was already in Form V.

"What d'you want?"

I turned over in bed with an effort. The book I had fallen asleep over fell with a bang to the floor. No, there was simply no getting away from it, you just couldn't read a novel anywhere in that hostel.

"Come along, Zhenya. . . ."

"Huh?"

"There's some man out there asking for you."

"What?"

I was out of bed in a trice. Without bothering to ask for details I thundered downstairs. My hands that had been doing up all my buttons automatically as I raced along, involuntarily clenched tight.

Where could the old scoundrel have sprung from? After all, it was not so long ago that I had read a damning article about him in the papers that was followed by a short announcement some time later to the effect that he had got three years. Three years couldn't possibly have passed. There was something fishy somewhere.

But when I strode outside there was a quite different figure waiting at the gate. That much I could see even from a distance. There was a nicely turned-out chap standing there in a leather jacket and a colourful checked shirt, with a camera slung over his shoulder and a beret perched on his head.

"But who could it be?" I said to myself taking a closer look as I deliberately slowed my pace down.

Meanwhile the man in the jacket beamed a smile at me that was so wide that it seemed to stretch from ear to ear. All of a sudden his face seemed to change shape and grow several times broader than it was long.

"Ko-o-olya!" I yelled, rushing over to him.

We greeted each other with a hug. It seemed an age since we'd last seen each other.

There he stood, Kolya Biryukov as ever was.

"Why didn't you come in?" I asked. "Surely you haven't forgotten the way? Come on in. You can't imagine how the lads'll. . . ."

"No," he said with a frown. "I can't. I'm very short of time. You see, I'm just stopping over between trains. Are you free now?"

"Me? Of course."

"Well, that's fine then."

He turned round and beckoned to a grey Volga taxi parked a short distance away. It obediently started its engine and drew up alongside.

"Where to?" I asked.

"To Kiev Station."

"Kiev Station?" I echoed in surprise. "But that's only a stone's throw away. We can go on foot." (It really was only a trifling distance, after all everything's within easy reach of our hostel.)

"In you get," said Kolya with a pat on the shoulder, as he opened the door for me. "There's very little time. I'm literally between trains."

Off we went and the first thing I asked was where he was off to.

"I'm on my way to Truskavets, to a sanatorium."

"What's the matter with you?" I asked casting a quick sideways glance at his stomach, for I had heard that people go to Truskavets to have stomach disorders treated. Just to think, a young chap like that. "Are you ill?"

"No," declared Kolya, brushing aside my fears. "It's just that our trade union committee had a spare holiday voucher that was about to go waste if no one took it. My leave was just coming up so I agreed to take it. They say it's as dull as ditchwater."

Five minutes later we were at Kiev Station. Kolya paid the driver and I noticed that he gave him a fifty-kopeck tip. He'd come a long way since the penniless hostel days!

We walked through the waiting room and into a restaurant, humming with people and filled with the sound of excited voices and the smell of fried onions. We sat down at a small table covered with a white tablecloth stiff with starch. There were spring flowers in the vase, daffodils I think.

"Well, how's life?" asked Kolya leaning over towards me, his chin propped up on his hands and his elbows on the table. "How are things?"

"OK," I replied. "Fine."

"Are you almost through with school now?"

"Yes, it's my last year."

"And what about?..." Kolya asked, flicking his finger at his throat. "Is it still there?"

"No," I replied with a shake of my head. "It disappeared a long time ago."

"I see. Where d'you go on to from here then?"

I shrugged. Of course I could have told Kolya about my intentions, let him in on my as yet tentative plans but.... I felt awkward and sheepish about wasting precious minutes on such trifles, particularly as Kolya had said that he had hardly any time left before his train. It was much more important to ask him about how life was treating him, about everything that had happened to him over all those years. I still couldn't come to somehow after the wonderful surprise of this unexpected meeting and believe that at that very moment there he was, Kolya Biryukov in person, sitting opposite me, Kolya Biryukov and none other, his elbows leaning on the table and a beam of a smile stretched from ear to ear, as if it was only yesterday that we had said good-bye.

But at that moment our conversation was interrupted by a waiter, asking for our order. Kolya opened the menu and after a quick glance at it asked for: "Two pickled herrings, two plates of borshch and two rissoles with vegetables."

Then he threw me a glance and again flicked his finger at his throat: "What about the other?" he asked.

"What?" I replied not catching on at first, but thinking he was asking me about my voice again. Then I realised he was asking about drink not voices.

"No," I said, feeling a shade embarrassed.

"No? All right, then I won't either. We won't have anything to drink," Kolya added to the waiter standing there with his pencil at the ready. "Just a bottle of lemonade."

"But how are you getting on?" I asked after the waiter had gone away to see to our order. "Are you still in the same place?"

"Yes. Life is treating me proud. I've been there for four years now and I'm getting the extra allowance for working up North too. And you know, Zhenya, I'm chairman of our trade union committee, at the fur farm."

"You're joking!" I said, unable to believe my ears.

"No, honest to God, I've just been elected to the post."

I sat there, blinking in astonishment, still finding it hard to believe that Kolya was chairman of a trade union committee. It's amazing how much responsibility is given to young people. Now one really could think of Kolya as Nikolai Ivanovich!

Our plates of borshch arrived. It was red, hot and smelt out of this world. No ordinary borshch, dish fit for a king!

"And how's your dog?" I asked next.

"Pon?" Kolya said, bringing out his wallet. He took out a photograph and handed it to me. From the photograph a mischievous dog was looking up at me with his tongue hanging out: he was white with black patches, very shaggy and for some reason bore a slight resemblance to Kolya himself! A first-class dog.

"I took that photo myself," Nikolai explained patting the leather case of his camera. Then he brought out another photo from his wallet and as he handed it to me, said: "Here's another one, that I took too."

The second photo showed a girl I had never seen before. Her eyes were almond-shaped and she had high cheek-bones and a wide smile and she too looked a bit like Kolya.

"Who's that?" I asked.

"That's Lyuba, my wife," came the reply.

Each minute brought a bigger surprise than the one before. Out they tumbled—chairman of the trade union committee, my wife . . . whatever next?

"Why isn't she going to Truskavets with you?"

"She can't travel at the moment," Kolya replied. "You see, we're expecting . . . a son or a daughter soon."

This piece of news even Kolya himself seemed to find a bit unnerving. The tips of his enormous ears turned several shades pinker. But perhaps it wasn't so much embarrassment as pride and happiness.

There was no doubt about it, opposite me was a really happy person, a real adult in view of all the things he had just been telling me, yet at the same time not quite—the tips of his ears could still turn pink. But at any rate he was definitely someone who had chosen his path in life, knew what he wanted and where he was going.

As for me. . . . Could I now start telling my old

friend about my dreams, my hopes and plans for the future? I felt a strong urge to do so, because he was the only person in whom I could really confide. I wanted to explain to him that I just couldn't envisage life without music. Look at Beethoven, he had not been able to live without music even after he had gone deaf, or Scriabin who had written his "Prelude for the Left Hand" —even if he had lost both hands he would have found some way of getting at the piano keys and they would never have let him down!

I'll tell you one thing, if I was to start from the very beginning, go back a hundred years and know in advance that I would set out from sleepy little Lipetsk to Moscow and first be the happy owner of a first-rate voice and then be miserable after I'd lost it—even if I had known all that in advance and been able to make my own decisions I would still have set out on that path, there would have been no other!

I was already quite determined to take up music after school. I too had hopes for the future and plans were starting to take shape in my mind. I wanted to tell Kolya Biryukov all about them very badly.

Yet I couldn't quite bring myself to do it. I was frightened lest Kolya Biryukov might react in the way people sometimes do after bitter disappointments: they don't want to look back to a world where things didn't work out for them, except to pour derision over it. That was what decided me against telling him about my plans in the end.

By now we'd got to the next course. In front of us were rissoles with fried potatoes and slices of salted cucumber. What wonderful food they served in the Kiev Station restaurant!

"Well, and how's Vladimir Konstantinovich?" inquired Kolya.

I listened carefully to the tone of voice in which Kolya asked that question and just to be sure I looked up at his face too. Was there any note of grudging or bitterness in his voice? No, nothing of the kind, genuine interest was clearly all that lay behind the question.

"He's fine," I said. "Working away. He gets ill sometimes though, his liver's been playing him up."

"His liver?" exclaimed Kolya. "It's livers that people go and have treated in Truskavets. He needs to go to one of their sanatoriums. For God's sake, there they go sending vouchers to places where nobody needs or wants them and I'm having to go there although I'm sure I'm going to be bored stiff."

"You must pop in and see him on your way home," I advised him. "Do go and see Vladimir Konstantinovich. You know how he is, to this day he feels bad about your desperate disappearing act."

I considered it best not to go into some other escapades that had added to the director's grey hairs.

"Well . . . perhaps I will go and see him," said Nikolai after thinking it over for a moment. "But on the way back. I'll have lots of things to get done then. . . . By the way, Zhenya," he inquired adopting a serious voice all of a sudden, "you don't know by any chance what the piano situation is in Moscow, do you?"

"Piano situation?"

"What I mean is, can you just go in and buy a piano or d'you have to put your name down on a waiting list?"

"I don't know, I'm afraid," I replied. "That wasn't something of immediate concern to me. But why?"

"I want to get one."

"What d'you need it for?"

"It's not really for me," said Nikolai, and again the tips of his ears went red. "It's not for me but for our son or daughter . . . whichever it'll be."

"Oh, I see."

"Yes," said Kolya. "Up where we live, we haven't got a music school yet, but I'll be able to teach him or her myself. I'll be all right for a start. I haven't forgotten a thing." Then he leant over the table towards me and fixing me with a penetrating look repeated: "I haven't forgotten a thing, anything at all."

But at that moment a voice rang out over the restaurant loudspeaker asking passengers for Lvov to hurry along to the platform. That was the train Kolya had to take and so we hastily downed our lemonade and went out to the platform.

5

I could picture it as clearly as if I had been an eyewitness. I could see little boys and girls perfectly innocent of any crime being led out to their death, to the gas chamber, to the terrible crematorium in Treblinka. I could see the terrible cloud of smoke rising up from the chimneys in a black pillar.

I could see the SS men in their helmets and dirty boots with rifles slung over their shoulders walking along on each side of that column of helpless children. Then at the front of the column

I could see Janusz Korczak, the teacher and friend of those children whom he accompanied on their last journey. In front of them there rose up a thick column of smoke and the children had already grasped everything. They knew that any minute now they would no longer be alive on this earth but adding fuel to that black smoke.

O Heavens, why was I born too late? Why wasn't I born twenty years earlier, so that I would have been in time to take part in the last war. Why didn't I have a single dead nazi to my credit and have to be content with those my father killed?

Worrying about that isn't going to get me anywhere though.

The reason these things were preying on my mind was because I decided at that stage to write an opera, a children's opera. I knew only too well that I would soon be leaving the school, the building where I had spent ten years of my life and I wanted to leave behind me something to be remembered by: I wanted to leave something to the small boys who would follow on after me.

When I started casting around for a suitable subject, I remembered how two years before when I had been in charge of the third-form Young Pioneer detachment one day I had read the boys Korczak's *King Matthew*, as we sat and basked on the bank of the river Protva. I read to them all about the boy-king Matthew, his friend Felek and the little Negro girl Klu-Klu.

It was a wonderful book and the little chaps sat there spellbound, their mouths slightly open in a mixture of indignation and fear as they followed Matthew on his way right through the city, where he was tied to a pillar in the square before an open pit and a troop of soldiers started loading their rifles. They heaved enormous sighs of relief when Matthew's death sentence was commuted to exile on an uninhabited island.

After I had shut the book I looked at those small boys and all of a sudden my hair stood up on end at the thought that it was children just like those snippet third-formers sitting there on the bank in nothing but little shorts, all sunburnt and covered in sand, whom the nazis had led under an armed escort to the gas chambers, whom they had led out in the direction of that black column of smoke. . . .

That thought shattered me so much that I must confess it made it impossible for me to tell the little boys about Janusz Korczak himself and about the fate of his charges. Probably though, I should have done. Yes, of course, I should have told them the whole story.

So now I had decided to write an opera entitled "King Matthew". It was not going to be a straightforward opera, but for want of a better expression a "double" opera. I planned to use the fairy-tale events from the book, while running parallel to them, or rather contrapuntally, there would be the real-life tragedy which took place in Treblinka. That was how it was to be: I was quite convinced that this was exactly how the subject should be approached.

The snag I came up against was the lyrics since Janusz Korczak's book was written in prose and the words would have to be adapted in verse form for the opera. Who would do that? That was something I hadn't got the slightest clue about and as far as I knew there was no one in our school who wrote poetry. But I decided to leave that problem to later and I got down to the music without any text. The first was a joyous introductory one to take the place of an overture, and the second a requiem in memory of those child martyrs. Both the chorales were for children's voices and if I do write the opera (as I'm determined to do) our boys singing those chorales will be enough to overwhelm anyone who hears them.

I used to work on them in the evenings. The problem there was that instruments were in very short supply. There were plenty of instruments all right but not enough rooms to contain them. They were squashed into all the classrooms, and you could find them in all the corridors and there was even one corridor where there were two pianos at opposite ends that were occasionally played on simultaneously. Everyone had to practice and there were so many boys in the school. Sometimes you got monotonous scales at one end of the corridor and a Mozart sonata at the other. Two boys would play away simultaneously trying not to listen to each other, which, of course, proved quite impossible! The result was utter chaos instead of music all because of the shortage of rooms.

That was why I used to wait till the evenings, by which time everyone would have had their fill of playing and be setting off exhausted for bed. Then my turn would come. I would sit at the grand piano armed with a manuscript book and pencils which I laid out on the music rest. Then I would start playing and noting things down.

My work was a constant search. Sometimes it would last a long time, but I usually found what I was looking for in the end, and would hastily jot down what I had lighted upon in the empty staves in front of me. The old building was filled with unfamiliar quiet at that time and outside the cold winter night made everything stand out in clear black and white, like the piano keys.

One night I heard steps coming down the corridor and wondered who on earth it could be at that late hour. Who on earth would still be around other than myself? Polina Romanovna perhaps? But it was unusual for her to come up to the first floor and those weren't her steps either. They slowed down at the door and then it opened a crack. I got up.

"Sit down, sit down. So you're burning the midnight oil, are you? I thought it must be you."

Vladimir Konstantinovich was wearing a heavy winter coat and a round hat with a velvet crown and he was carrying a knotted stick. Surely he couldn't have only just left work? He must have come back for something he'd forgotten. It was a way he had. Or perhaps he'd been out for a bit of night air and seen the lighted window and come to make sure everything was all right.

He sat down on the chair next to the grand piano, took off his winter hat and unbuttoned his collar.

"Come now, let me have a peep."

I obediently handed him a page. After all he already knew that I was trying my hand at writing music and he knew about the opera. He knew everything there was to know about us boys, all our little secrets.

"This is a chorale, isn't it?" he asked as his eyes sped across the page from left to right and at the same time travelled up and down. "Hm-m-m. . . ." He started to hum the top part and then the fourth one: it was a six-part chorale.

"Hm-m-m."

"No good?" I asked straight out.

"What makes you think that? Not bad at all. There's a good deal of interesting stuff here."

Once again he started to scrutinise the page before him and then commented:

"Only you see, my boy, here things seem to split up into two: here you've got the right hand, here you've got the left, you can see at once that you've been working at a piano. But choral music is a completely different proposition. You must conceive the whole thing differently. After all you have sung in a choir."

Yes, I had, I'd sung in a choir all right and sung on my own without the others too. But all that was way back in the past. I sat there looking down at the floor.

"That's nothing to get depressed about!" said Vladimir Konstantinovich with a laugh. "No great failing. You're not the only person to have made this bloomer. Take Scriabin's First Symphony, the chorale part in that doesn't come off. People sing away all right, but it's not choral music."

Once again I lowered my head, for I couldn't bear to hear people blaspheme like that, to hear anyone find fault with Scriabin.

"Now his 'Prometheus' is quite a different matter. There the choral part is first-class!" the old man said, taking pity on me and Scriabin after all. "And you know, Zhenya, I actually saw him and heard him play. Yes, it was back in 1911 at the first performance of 'Prometheus'. Kusevitsky was conducting and Scriabin was playing the piano part. He looked very small, or at least so it seemed from where I was up in the gods, for it was the days when I was still a student at the Conservatoire. How he played, Zhenya, how he played! It wasn't as if there was all that actual force in his playing, like Rakhmaninov's, for instance, but his dramatic passages sent shivers down your spine."

He was bending down towards me as he spoke and I could clearly make out the criss-cross network of tiny red veins in his eyes which seemed to get thicker as he reminisced.

To think that he'd actually listened to Scriabin playing! I'd never have thought he was so old.

Then he turned to me and asked if I had anything new I'd written for the piano: "Come on, bring out the opus."

I opened my music case and handed the opus to him, an invention I had written the week before which I was very pleased with myself.

Once more Vladimir Konstantinovich started to peruse my pages intently and then came out with another "hm-m-m-m".

"What is it? Is that no good either?" I was sunk to the depths of despair by that time.

"Why, d'you think I know?"

Once again he leant over towards me with a conspiratorial air and said:

"What makes you think I know everything? For I don't, you know!" He then proceeded to undo another button of his thick winter coat and pulled off his scarf. "Choral music, now that I do know something about, and how to make worthwhile people out of you rapscallions is also something up my street, although I don't always bring it off..." he added with a sigh.

I immediately guessed what he was referring to. Not long before a boy from Form IX had got himself drunk on vodka. He had just gone and bought a bottle of vodka and drunk the whole thing, just to see what it was like. What had that got to do with me though?

"Get me straight, Zhenya. What you've written

 there is too serious for me to be able to judge properly. It's more than a question of a mark to be put down in the school register. Here you need to turn to someone else for an opinion. Know what? Why don't you go and see Him?"

He didn't mention the Him by name but I realised at once whom he was getting at.

"Yes, go and see him. Show him what you've done and play him some. I'll give you his telephone number straight away." Vladimir Konstantinovich opened his coat and started hunting through his pocket. Then he stopped half-way after apparently changing his mind.

"No, that's probably not the way to go about it. He's always giving people the slip—he has to find time to write music in. I'll telephone him myself."

* * *

It's probably unnecessary to mention the fact that I arrived at the address in question an hour ahead of the appointed time. That way I could make quite sure of not being late. But it would have been inconsiderate to come to a strange house before I was expected. There was nothing for it but to wait.

I spent the best part of an hour twiddling my thumbs in the courtyard of the house where the composer lived. It was a house where I had heard all the inhabitants were composers, so that it was easier for them to visit each other and get together for all kinds of meetings. It looked as if the children playing around in that yard were all composers' children too. I'd never seen as wild a group of kids anywhere. I spent a whole hour just watching their antics. There was no end to the things they thought up.

Opposite the porchways there was a long row

of cars. They were obviously not being used at the moment, probably because the winter had turned out to be a very cold one. Starting up cars in that weather would have been a real problem. There was a thick layer of snow covering all the roofs and the wheels were buried in deep drifts, which had probably been made by the street-sweepers as they went about their work.

Round those cars there was a whole crowd of well-dressed children having the time of their lives. They were taking runs at those private cars, clambering up on the roofs and then sliding down again on their bottoms. Admittedly some of those cars were old Pobedas and Moskviches of some antediluvian vintage. I didn't feel sorry for those at all. At the end of the row, though, there was a Volga: although it too was covered by a deep blanket of snow, you could still see that the car was brand-new and the very latest model. It was a pure miracle, and that glistening brand-new car was also being used as a slide by those spoilt brats.

I was so horrified that I felt like giving them a real telling off and shooing them away with a box or two on the ear for good measure. But then I changed my mind: I suddenly had a mental picture of a window being opened high up in the building somewhere, while I was in the middle of administering the overdue punishment and a father's angry face leaning out and saying: "What d'you think you're doing down there, you good-for-nothing, don't you lay a finger on my boy! It's my car anyway. Let the child have his fun. Who d'you think you are anyway? Militia! Where's the militia?!"

No, the devil take them. I wasn't going to get involved. Anyway I only had five more minutes left to go before my appointment now. I went up in the lift and rang at the door.

He opened the door to me himself. "Please come in. I'm very glad to see you."

It even looked as if he really was glad to see me, that welcoming smile made me feel like an old friend. It looked the kind of smile that came right from the heart, not one that was donned just to keep up appearances.

"Do take your coat off and hang it up over here."

Normally, I would have described the flat in minute detail. It would have been interesting for anyone to know what kind of home the composer had, me in particular, because heaven knows if I'd ever find myself in that flat again. But I hardly saw anything. The master of the house led me straightaway to his study without taking me into any of the other rooms on the way, or parading them as we went. Even in that study I didn't really notice anything, apart from the grand piano and the man himself.

I was horribly nervous, beset by blind panic. I was well aware of the importance of that meeting for my future career and I didn't notice anything around me.

I looked up at Him and He looked down at me through his glasses with their very thick lenses that seemed to transfix me.

"So I hear you're about to leave the choir school," he said, "and you've been writing some music. Well, let's start with some music then, shall we? That's the simplest way to go about things now, isn't it? Don't you think?"

I nodded in agreement. I also thought that music was the simplest thing to understand on this earth.

"Take a seat," He said inviting me to come over

to the piano. I had thought that he would start off by looking at my chorales, which Vladimir Konstantinovich had poured so much cold water on. But I didn't dare suggest that and meekly did as I was told.

I sat down at the piano.

"Well what are we going to hear?"

" 'Nona-waltz', Etude," I said starting to list my repertoire, " 'Basso ostinato', Invention."

"We'll have the Invention," He commanded.

I wiped my damp palms on my trousers and poised them at the ready over the keyboard. But just at that moment the telephone rang. That would happen. Life's like that. Fate. . . .

"Forgive me," He said and went over to the telephone. "Oh, hallo!" He said and was soon immersed in talking shop with a fellow composer. Well, even that had its advantages. It would be something to relate to my grandchildren. "What? But of course I was there. It was astounding! Quite incredible!"

I pricked up my ears.

"Inspiration. But of course, yet it wasn't only a matter of inspiration, first and foremost a question of skill. He's quite simply a genius. My dear chap, I tell you there's no one on a par with him anywhere in the world."

I was fidgeting around on the piano-stool from astonishment. Just fancy that! And I had come hopping along confident that the man in whose flat I was about to play my pieces was the most gifted of them all. I had been convinced that there was no one on a par with the man talking on the telephone a few steps away from me.

"Yes, that second goal. The way he took the puck at that close angle! I've never seen anything like it!"

The conversation went on for another couple of minutes. Then He put down the receiver and gave an apologetic shrug, saying: "Excuse the interruption."

He walked over to the window. He seemed completely taken up with the conversation he had just had.

"This is my Invention," I reminded him.

"Yes, yes. Do start," he replied.

I started playing, concentrating hard as I went because it was a very difficult piece although I had composed it myself. Nevertheless I managed not just to keep track of my own fingers but of his reactions as well. He was standing by the window with his back to me. Suddenly He tensed his back and squared his shoulders. He put his face right up against the window-pane which started to mist over from his angry breathing.

I clenched my teeth in a fury. I realised now what it was all about. By this time all my doubts had been dispelled. I was quite sure who the brand-new Volga out in the yard belonged to. I knew very well what encouraging sight down below was greeting the gaze of the man to whom I was playing my Invention.

If only I'd had the courage of my convictions and shooed away those boys as they deserved and boxed their ears into the bargain. Now, thanks to them, everything was going up in smoke. I might as well stop playing, get up and go.

I went on playing though, because I had just got to the most important part of the Invention and my fingers were so firmly caught up in the strands of the music that I probably would have found it quite impossible to tear them away from the keys.

All of a sudden He was standing there next

to me, with his elbows planted on the grand piano, looking straight at me. I hadn't even noticed Him move away from the window, but now He was here and I could feel the steady gaze of those glasses. It was almost as if He was using them to listen with as well.

He went on listening and I knew that He would go on listening for as long as I chose to play, even if out there in the yard someone chose to turn his car wheels uppermost.

He listened and I played on, stepping up the pace for fear that the telephone might ring before I got to the end. But I could sense even that wouldn't distract Him now. . . .

6

"Zhenya, Zhenya!"

With an enormous effort I managed to open one eye and look out, still through a haze of dreams. Of course, who could it have been but the one and only Zhenya Usachov.

"Get lost," I said and turned over on to my other side.

"But, Zhenya!" he called, starting to shake my shoulder.

Oh, for Heaven's sake, why won't anyone let me get some proper sleep? After all I've completed my course at the choir school now: not just in my dreams, but for real, and tomorrow I'll be taking the entrance exams for a place at the Conservatoire, starting with the most important one, composition, to be followed by a whole load of others. I'd been up poring over my books all night and must have fallen asleep by accident: sure enough there was my harmony text-book under my cheek.

I couldn't have been asleep more than a couple of hours and my head was going round in circles. No, I wasn't going to get up for anything. I lunged out with a heel at random but didn't hit my target. By that time the ubiquitous pest was tugging away at my other shoulder.

"Zhenya, but Zhenya!"

The brat! It was always him that woke me up. It was always bound to be Usachov and no other. It was impossible to shake him off. Where did he sprung from this time? What was he doing in Moscow, when he should have been out at the Young Pioneer camp: it was over a month ago that the boys from the junior classes had set out for Vereya. Everyone had long since gone their separate ways and the hostel was deserted. Vladimir Konstantinovich made a generous exception for us school-leavers who were preparing for the exams to get into the Conservatoire and the Gnesin Music Institute: we were allowed to stay on at the hostel although officially we were no longer part of the school and entitled to do so.

But what was it that had brought Zhenya Usachov along this time? Had he run away from the Young Pioneer camp, perhaps? I wouldn't put that past him. Oh, but of course, I'd quite forgotten in that exhausted sleep: they were coming home that day from the Young Pioneer camp, the whole jolly lot of them.

Yes, if you please, they were going abroad, to Poland. They had been invited to some children's music festival. Work had been started on new suits for the occasion a good six months ago. They had been swatting up Polish songs at singing practice for over three months. They had things up their sleeves to curry favour with the Polish audiences. Zhenya Usachov would be doing the solos: it was he now who was the choir's leading soloist, Nikolai Biryukov's and Zhenya Prokhorov's successor. So off they were going abroad... the lucky devils. In the old days there had been no such gallivanting, we had stayed at home. Those little tiddlers were heading for foreign lands.

"Come on, Zhenya, d'you hear? Up you get!"

Wait a minute, I'll give you "going abroad" if you don't look out! I leapt to my feet and shouted:

"What d'you want?"

"There's a lady out there asking for you."

"What kind of lady?"

"Dunno... this kind." At that he started to paint a mime portrait of my visitor. First came a rose-bud mouth, then he traced arched eyebrows and for the finishing touch outlined her figure with a flowing movement out—in—out. What d'you know, a mere fifth-former!

"I don't know any ladies like that," I said and flopped down on the bed again, closing my eyes tight shut.

"But she's asking for you. She asked me to go and call Zhenya Prokhorov."

I was only playing it cool really. As I lay there with my eyes shut I started trying to guess who it might be. Maya Vyazemskaya? Perhaps she'd come to her senses and repented? Perhaps she was here to make amends? I couldn't care less. I'd got over all that long since. It was all over, all finished with. What was more, I'd heard not long ago from Georgi that Maya had gone down South to the Artek Young Pioneer camp, so she couldn't possibly be in Moscow. But who else could it be? Surely it wasn't the red-haired girl whom I'd met at Georgi's party and kissed after I'd taken her home all the way to Noviye Kuzminki. Surely she hadn't turned up all of a sudden. How was I going to get out of that one? A quick get-away through the back entrance perhaps, and then over the fence and into the Zoo. I knew the way like the palm of my hand.

"Zhenya, do come along," whined Usachov into my ear.

Oh well, I suppose I'd have to pull myself together. After all I was a real adult by now. I was already in possession of a certificate, complete with a seal bearing a coat of arms, and the proud owner of an identity card. Here I was, about to try for a place at the Conservatoire. Surely I wasn't afraid of something as unimportant as some red-head or other. Well, so we had kissed. So what? She may well have kissed other people as well as me. I was quite capable of standing up for myself.

"Zhenya."

"Give over," I said in an angry voice and resolved once and for all to get up. I didn't have to waste time dressing for I had gone to sleep and woken up again fully dressed, complete with shirt and trousers. All I had to do was do up my sandals, give my face a splash of cold water and run a comb through my hair.

A moment later I went downstairs and walked over to the gate with that nonchalant air you always see in Westerns when cowboys know that at the gate old friends are waiting for them, each with a pistol in their pocket. I too casually stuck my hands in my pockets.

At the gate was fluttering something dazzlingly white, so much it was enough to make you blink. It was a white dress, the kind people wear at school-leavers' balls, or buy in shops for brides and bridegrooms. It was as if one kiss in a porchway was enough to make people turn up for you in a wedding dress and whisk you off to the Palace of Weddings in a taxi waiting just round the corner, a White Maria.

However, as I walked over to the gate my fears gradually subsided. I was soon quite sure that it wasn't the red-head from Noviye Kuzminki, because the girl in the gateway had quite different hair. Nor was it Maya, it just wasn't. Soon I felt absolutely calm for there in the gateway was a girl I had never set eyes on before. She was a rather pretty, shapely girl in a dazzlingly white dress and I could have sworn I'd never seen her before. That meant she didn't constitute any direct danger for me now.

I felt this even more when she met me with a very timid, shy smile and waited until I had got right up to her before saying "Hallo, Zhenya." At that she stretched out her hand which I duly shook, adding "Hi!"

"You probably don't recognise me?" she inquired.

"What makes you think that," I replied. "On the contrary." May I be forgiven if I'd ever seen her anywhere.

"I recognised you at once, although you've changed very much," she went on and then asked if I thought she had changed a lot.

"Not at all," I assured her. "Not in the slightest."

She gave me a searching look and her lips trembled a fraction. Surely she wasn't going to cry, that would have been the last straw. But no, she smiled again and said:

"I thought you wouldn't recognise me. I'm Sasha Tiunova from Lipetsk. D'you remember?"

* * *

We were walking down into the centre from the Lenin Hills. Beneath us was the Moskva River and to the left where the bank of the river juts out in a broad curve there was the crater of the Luzhniki Stadium. A hollow roar rose up from it which meant that there was probably a football match going on with half of Moscow watching it, as today was Sunday. On the right near the Neskuchny Gardens the other half of Moscow was frying itself in the sun and splashing about in the water. Straight ahead of us at the far side of the bridge we could see the bright flags of the Luzhniki Fair fluttering in the breeze: there was an enormous crowd of people coming and going there too, Moscow's third half, the people who are just passing through or who come up to Moscow for the day.

Walking along at my side, leaning backwards a fraction as she made her way down the steep hill, was another temporary guest to the city, Sasha Tiunova. We were on our way back from the parapet on the brow of the Lenin Hills where we had had a long talk. Sasha had put me in the picture about everything. She had come to Moscow on a special excursion and was now working as a lab assistant in the Lipetsk silicates plant. This year she had completed evening school and, as I had guessed, she had made a hit at the school-leavers' ball in that very same white dress. Zina Gvozdeva, she said, was training to become a nurse. She also told me that Vera Ivanovna was dead.

I, in my turn, told Sasha Tiunova everything there was to tell her about me. I told her everything just as it was, in broad outlines of course. It was already after three o'clock and I was ravenous, not having had any breakfast: my companion was bound to be pretty hungry by this time as well after all the walking we'd been doing. There were still a few coins tinkling in my pocket and as we came into Komsomolsky Prospekt I invited Sasha into a youth café. I knew that they sold highly-spiced kebabs in there and at reasonable prices. Sasha readily agreed and in we went. The café was fairly empty and we sat down at a table near the window.

On the platform at the far end there were already some young chaps in red shirts laying on music despite the fact that it was not yet four o'clock. There were five of them: clarinet, saxophone, bass guitar, piano and drums. They were playing George Gershwin's "Man I Love" but after some ten bars for some reason the music stopped and they started from the beginning again. I realised that this wasn't the real thing yet, they were just practising their repertoire for the evening show in the presence of munching customers. Perhaps there was no other suitable place for them to practice. They were very young and all in red shirts.

I must confess I don't really like small amateur jazz groups like that. I like the big stuff with more brass, like our Oleg Lundstrem's band for instance, and when it comes to foreign groups I was impressed by Benny Goodman who visited Moscow not long ago.

Our waitress brought us two glasses of punch complete with drinking straws. It was very tasty although not very dear. There was a great heap of ice at the bottom so that while you drank the glass didn't seem to get any emptier as the ice gradually melted.

Once again the red-shirts interrupted their music only to take up the tune again at the same place. On you go, polish it up!

"Zhenya," started up Sasha, looking at me hard, "why didn't you answer my letter? I wrote to you, you know. Did you get it?"

"Yes, in fact, I kept the letter. I've still got it hidden away somewhere."

"Why didn't you answer it then?"

"Why didn't I answer? I meant to. I kept on meaning to, but just didn't get round to it."

"Why?"

"I don't remember. Something happened at the time that stopped me answering."

"What was it?" Sasha asked.

I frowned in concentration as I tried to remember what it had been. "I can't remember. All I know is that something happened, but what I can't for the life of me remember. It was all a long time ago."

"You don't seem to remember anything," said Sasha. "You have a very bad memory."

"No, I have a good memory," I countered. "When it comes to music I have a really good memory but these last few days I've been swatting till I can't think straight. Perhaps I've been overdoing it."

"Have you got an exam tomorrow?"

"Yes, tomorrow."

The café was gradually filling up. Some other young fellows of about my age had come in with their girl-friends in tow too. They started ordering punches as well. Then an unshaven man tottered in, downed a glass of spirits at the bar and tottered out again. But for the most part the clients were young chaps on their own or in groups, who were probably on their way back from the football match (the stadium was only just round the corner). They sat down round the little tables and ordered Zhiguli beer. Being without their own girls they started brashly looking over the ones that happened to be sitting there in that café.

My companion, I noticed, attracted a great deal of those brash looks. Perhaps it was because Sasha was in a white dress that she stood out in the crowd, looking as if she had just come from a ball or was on her way to get married.

Outside in the street odd people would draw even with our table that was right by the window, stop in their tracks as if they were glued to the spot and start patting their pockets as if to say: where have my cigarettes and matches disappeared to, I could do with a smoke.

What rotters they all were. To hell with all those football fans and budding Petrosyans. What did they see in her after all? I didn't find her so very out of the ordinary. Blow me if I did!

"Zhenya, you know I lied to you."

"What d'you mean 'lied'?"

"About coming to Moscow on an excursion. I'm not here on an excursion at all."

Taken aback at that unexpected news I started poking the last scraps of melting ice at the bottom of my glass avoiding Sasha's gaze for the moment. To be honest though, the news hadn't been as unexpected as all that. I'd already had a feeling that she hadn't come on an excursion. It is hard to imagine anyone who'd come to Moscow on an excursion to have been there that long without having been taken up to see the view down over the city from the Lenin Hills. That's the first place visitors are always taken too. And there was no doubt that it had been the first time she'd ever seen that view when I'd showed it to her that afternoon. That was what had made me think she must have come to Moscow for some other reason than just to see the sights. I hadn't expected her admission so soon though.

"Two more glasses of punch," I said to the waiter.

All this time the chaps in red shirts were still playing Gershwin's "Man I Love". By now, though, they were getting along without any hitches. They no longer had to keep on retracing their tracks. Either they'd already finished practising, or they'd got so carried away that they'd forgotten they were meant to be practicing and that it was not yet time to put on their evening performance! They'd just got carried away with the strong rhythm, the haunting tune and played on and on, letting the various players in turn come forward to solo. Yes that's the beauty of those little jazz groups, the freedom, the scope for improvisation. Gershwin's "Man I Love" was in its own way a woman's confession of love.

Surely she couldn't have been remembering me all those years. Of course when my record had come out and the song was continually being churned out over the radio, of course you'd remember. But afterwards, when my singing days were over, what was there to remind her of me then? Or perhaps the very fact of my disappearance, the new silence, made her think of me, worried her and led her to come all the way to Moscow to look for me? Perhaps I really was that important to her? There's something very pleasant about the knowledge that someone on this earth actually needs you. But could it really be that from that ridiculously young age. . . .

"Zhenya," Sasha went on with a serious look in her eyes. "I know what you must have been thinking just now, but it's not true."

"What d'you mean 'it's not true'?" I asked in surprise. "You yourself said just now. . . ."

"You got me wrong. I said that I hadn't come to Moscow on an excursion and you went and imagined. . . ." At that she turned to look out of the window and her lips quivered a tiny bit like they had before that morning. But she started to smile again and went on: "I didn't want to tell you, but I too came here to take my entrance exams. I tried for the Engineering Institute but I boshed it. I ploughed the very first exam. There's no point in going on because I wouldn't be able to collect up the necessary points now whatever happened."

"Where d'you go from here then?"

"That's it. I go back to Lipetsk and I'll go on working where I was before. Then next year I'll try again."

So that was how things stood. I must confess I was a little disappointed. No, nothing to do with all that other business . . . just at the thought that Sasha Tiunova wouldn't be able to enter the Engineering Institute this September.

"Well, that's really hard luck, but you're taking it well," I said cheerfully, trying to jolly her along a bit. "If I fail tomorrow, too, I'll come along to Lipetsk with you. I'll start working at your factory. Would they take me?"

"No. They wouldn't."

"Why?"

"In the first place you have to do a training course first. . . ." (It was sick-making, there was nowhere on earth for a soul to go without doing some training or other.)

"... and in the second place you won't fail. You'll get in."

"How d'you know?"

"I just know," said Sasha.

On the quiet I touched the underneath of the wooden table. What was it that made her so sure? What had she to go on?

Then all of a sudden a feeling came over me rather like the one I had had when I had been sitting with Kolya Biryukov in the restaurant at the Kiev Station. I felt that opposite me was another mature person, who had found her path in life and knew where she was going. But on the first occasion I had been with Kolya Biryukov, or rather Nikolai Ivanovich, chairman of the local trade union committee and all. He had been older than me and more experienced and I had looked on him as one of my elders.

But here was a slip of a girl, my own age. What gave her the right to talk to me as if she was much older and more mature than I was? Surely it wasn't true after all, that women—even when they are miniature ones like that—are wiser than us men? Then I felt exactly the same urge come over me as I had experienced at the Kiev Station with Kolya Biryukov, I wanted to pour out everything to Sasha, tell her exactly how I felt.

I wanted to explain to her that if she proved right and I did get a place at the Conservatoire that was only half the battle, if that. Perhaps they would take me on, I'd do my homework and get my degree. That degree certificate would say precious little though: "Surname—Prokhorov. Qualification—Composer." My name would be on the certificate of course and the composer bit, but then I would have to start proving that I really was a composer and that would be when the fun started. After all some people go on and on trying to prove their talent, without ever being able to convince anybody.

Getting into the Conservatoire was only half the battle, if they can compose. I wanted to explain all this to Sasha but I decided against it, because it might so happen that things actually did turn out as Sasha had foreseen and I really would get a place. It would have been cruel to go into all those niceties, sitting there with someone who hadn't been accepted, who had already failed.

"What time is your exam?" she asked.

"At ten."

"May I come along?"

"Where to?"

"To the Conservatoire, to the Tchaikovsky statue. I could wait for you there tomorrow. OK?"

"OK," I nodded.

* * *

Through the thick July foliage and the bars of the Conservatoire railings I could see a white dress out there by the pedestal where Pyotr Tchaikovsky was enthroned, as we hung round the entrance waiting for ten o'clock.

The exam was to take place in the White Hall. White halls, white dresses—I interpreted the coincidence as a good sign.

Who would blame me for touching wood the day before, for putting my faith in white magic on the morning of the exam? It was all nonsense, of course, but on a day as momentous as this you involuntarily made sure that black cats crossed your path, avoided walking under ladders and added up the digits on your bus tickets to see if you had a lucky number. . . . What superstition does to people! When so much is at stake, superstition knows no bounds.

The chap with the bulging music case over there in the corner had caught my attention because of his beard, and I noticed how he kept on turning round to the wall to toss a coin, to see if it came down heads or tails.

There was only a quarter of an hour to go before the composition exam. Grey-haired men and women were starting to turn up—the wielders of our fate. There were some younger ones as well, without grey hair, but fate-wielders all the same. We would-be students stepped back to let them pass. Forming an aisle we stood there mumbling respectful "good mornings".

An especially awed hush fell over our assembly when He appeared: "Good morning, good morning, good morning. . . ."

"Good morning," he answered, with a slight bow of his head taking us all in with one round sweep of his spectacles.

I was standing near the front and he couldn't help but notice me. He noticed everyone, of course, and I was standing in a particularly prominent position. However, it looked as if he hadn't recognised me and that I found horribly offputting. But then I took heart, for I remembered another superstition: it was a good sign that he hadn't recognised me. That meant that I would be rich, and perhaps that I might be a student as well. Another thought also crossed my mind. It was quite possible that he was deliberately making it look as if he didn't know me. It would have never done for him, a member of the selection committee, to make it obvious for all and sundry that he was personally acquainted with one of the would-be entrants.

The whole crowd of us then moved over to go into the building. I looked round and sure enough Pyotr Tchaikovsky was still sitting there in his bronze armchair, his hand frozen in a gentle sweep as if he was bringing in the orchestra. At his feet a white dress was still fluttering in the breeze.

The first candidate to be called out for the exam was a wee mouse of a girl. Benign smiles followed her into the examination room, not because of her diminutive size but because everyone knew perfectly well that since time immemorial, in the whole history of music, there has never been a composer of genius among the fair sex. For some reason women don't seem to have made the grade in this particular quarter. Everywhere else in our country matriarchy seems to be the order of the day, but when it comes to composing at least, we men still stand a fair chance.

The chap with the beard and the bulging music case came over to me and asked: "What have you brought along?"

"Nothing much," I replied in a rather pathetic voice: "An étude, a waltz."

"I see," replied the other fellow in sympathetic tones.

"And what about you?" I inquired for politeness' sake.

"I've got a symphony here," answered Beard and then added: "My second."

That meant that he must have failed when he presented his first symphony the year before. Oh, well, never mind: he'd make it with his fifth. Fifth symphonies as a rule make the grade.

The walls in the Conservatoire were solid ones, the kind they always built in the old days. The doors and the windows also shut properly. Even so, although we couldn't actually hear anything, we could sense with every nerve that the whole building was brimming over with music, the high trills of violins, the pensive ripples of bassoons, cascading piano music, murmuring harps and peals of song. Exams were going on on every floor, in every hall and room. Those old hallowed walls were bursting out at the seams with music.

Out scampered the little mouse, her face radiant with happiness. But surely not... surely time-honoured traditions hadn't crumbled?

Then the stern-looking woman with a pince-nez, who called people in to the exam-room, came out holding a list of candidates in her hand and read out the next name.

Beard lowered his head as if he was about to charge and moved over to the door. After that a fellow in an embroidered Ukrainian tunic, no longer in his first youth, came over to me (Heaven knows why they all kept on coming over to talk to me, of all people?) and said: "I've brought songs along. D'you think I've got any hope, with songs I mean?"

His eyes were filled with desperate longing and I immediately answered: "But why on earth not? Songs are very important."

"But songs, that's all I've got.... What d'you think?"

"Everything'll be quite all right," I assured him, looking at his intricately embroidered tunic. After all, why shouldn't he be accepted on the strength of his songs? There was no reason at all why they shouldn't take him, provided they were decent songs, as long as they weren't filled with the same desperate longing you could see in his eyes.

Twenty minutes later Beard appeared. They'd given him a long run for his money. He had brought them a symphony after all. But the expression on his face left no room for doubt as regards the accuracy of my forecast. He should have started out with a Fifth. I felt sorry for the fellow. . . .

Who would be the next to go in, I wondered. Just in case I looked over to the window to see if Tchaikovsky and the white frock were still in place. Everything was as it should be.

The woman in the pince-nez took another look at her list and read out:

"Prokhorov, Yevgeni."

